EVERY

JULIENNE'S STORY . . .

What did it matter if I wasn't Miss Popularity like Blair? I could get by without things like football games and proms and high school boys, I told myself. All I needed was my imagination and books like DARK FLOWER OF LOVE and RAGING TIDE OF PASSION.

But the dream world that Julienne reads about in historical romance novels *isn't* enough for her, anymore . . . not since she met Peter—a real live boy who's *very* interested in her. If only love wasn't so hard in real life, though. If only she didn't have to worry about what Peter's friends thought of her, and if only she didn't have the sneaking suspicion that, deep down, Peter was more interested in helping her out of her shyness than in really loving her . . .

TWO BY TWO ROMANCES™ are designed to show you both sides of each special love story in this series. You get two complete books in one. Read what it's like for a girl to fall in love. Then turn the book over and find out what love means to the boy.

Julienne's story begins on page one of this half of ONLY A DREAM AWAY. Does Peter feel the same way? Flip the book over and read his story to find out.

4

TWO BY TWO
ROMANCE™

Only A Dream Away

Kathryn Makris

WARNER BOOKS

A Warner Communications Company

*To Gavin, my love and inspiration,
for believing.*

Only
A Dream Away

JULIENNE'S STORY

Chapter One

Lord Reynold had just swept Lady Eleanor into his arms. She was caught off guard. I was smiling. The sleeve of her blue velvet gown slipped a little off one of her slim shoulders, drawing Reynold's attention to the milky whiteness of her throat. She quivered in his embrace. I, Julienne Kelsey, shut my eyes and quivered with her.

I opened my eyes to see theirs meet. The dark, brooding power of Reynold's gaze melted my resistance. As his arms crushed Eleanor to him, I felt the rise and fall of my breathing. He was touching my lips . . .

It was a lousy time for the bell to ring.

But things like that were always happening. Real life, in general, had bad timing.

The entire seventh-period math class rose to its feet at once. Without bothering to mark my place, I whisked *Dark Flower of Love* into my tote bag. No one seemed to notice.

They were probably too busy thinking about the football game and the Friday night dates they were all rushing out to get ready for. None of them could have cared less about me.

They didn't notice me on the way to my locker, or at my locker, or in the halls on my way out. It didn't matter that I was wearing a billowy fuschia blouse and khaki riding pants. I could dress exactly like Lady Eleanor or even Bozo the Clown if I wanted, and no one would pay any attention. I was invisible.

Once in a while, if I was wearing something *really* different, like my hat with the long feather, I'd get a second glance or two. But for the most part, my five-foot-three, one-hundred-and-five-pound body just faded into the background. Not even my long auburn hair got much notice.

The truth is that kids at Frazier High had been ignoring me ever since I started there the year before. My mother's big promotion had meant that we had to move out of Portland into the little suburban town of Webber Falls right in the middle of tenth grade. I had just barely started to get used to being a sophomore at my old high school, when all of a sudden I was dropped into a new one, midyear.

That was when I gave up on Real Life. It sounds like a ridiculous thing to do, but at the time I felt that I had no choice. As hard as I tried to adapt to the changes that were always complicating my life, it never worked. The minute I got used to one change, another would pop up.

I think that's why my thoughts were always drifting off into historical romance novels, where there were things I could count on. The heroines were always beautiful and poised, and the heroes were always handsome and daring. They always ended up madly in love with each other. When I let myself float into *their* worlds, I didn't care what anyone thought of me, or whether I had any friends. I could dress to fit my mood, mumble to myself in the hallways, and ignore high school (just the way it ignored me). I didn't have to worry about being lonely and invisible.

"Julienne! Hi!" Blair Doran came up behind me as I left the classroom.

Well, maybe she was one person at Frazier who didn't ignore me. But I wasn't sure why.

"What're you up to this afternoon?" Her shining dark hair bounced around her head like Dorothy Hamill's.

"I'm going riding at the stables," I answered, wondering why she wasn't off having fun somewhere instead of bothering with me. She was cute and popular and had a terrific boyfriend. Just because our mothers were friends didn't mean she had to make it her personal mission in life to talk to me.

"Oh, yeah, it's your riding day. I forgot. Well, have a good time—see you at lunch on Monday."

"Thanks," I said, watching her walk back to Stephen Belsaw, who always seemed to be waiting for her.

As I was leaving the building, my mind slipped back to Lady Eleanor. The velvet folds of her gown followed her in whispers down the marble-paved hall. She walked swiftly toward the door beyond which fate awaited. I followed, step by step, down the sidewalk. The wind blew back my hair. The door flew open and a draft blew back Lady Eleanor's. We waited there together—she in the doorway, I at the Sutter Avenue bus stop.

It had all started years ago. Before my father got sick, I had always felt pretty average and normal. But when we lost him, I was suddenly a very different eight-year-old. His death was hard to accept. As a result, I started to pretend. I pretended that we still had my father. I pretended that my mother was a famous artist who supported us with her paintings, and not an unknown who had to go to work as a secretary. We didn't really have to move out of our house into an apartment, I imagined, and I didn't have to change

3

schools. All the while, those things were actually happening. And to make the situation worse, I skipped a grade of school along the way, so that I became known as a "smart kid." By the time we arrived in Webber Falls, I had little use for reality.

What did it matter if I wasn't Miss Popularity, like Blair? I could get by without things like football games and proms and high school boys, I told myself. All I needed was my imagination, and books like *Dark Flower of Love* and *Raging Tide of Passion*. At least, I was trying to convince myself that was all I needed. Deep down, I couldn't help wanting to break out and get to know people. To really *live* life. But I kept reminding myself that there was no sense in getting involved in things at Frazier High, when some change or other was bound to come along and ruin it all.

Besides, I had more important things to concentrate on, didn't I? My career as a writer, for one thing. My plan was to do more than just read about characters like Lady Eleanor and Lord Reynold. I was going to *create* them.

As I got on the big green bus, I pulled out the scrap of paper I had scrawled on yesterday while listening to the radio. *WRITING CONTEST. KWEB Public Radio Theater Hour. Looking for 30-minute scripts. Any subject. 1st, 2nd, 3rd prizes include typewriters. Performance on air.*

It was silly. Silly of me to even consider it. I did have the beginnings of a story at home, a beautiful story. But all the stories I wrote seemed beautiful to me, at first. Then, after a few days, when I looked at them again, I hated them. Besides, there would be hundreds of entries. Thousands. All submitted by writers much more talented than a fifteen-year-old who read historical romance novels.

And Mom, of course, would hit the roof, in her own way. "This is not the time for you to concentrate your energies on writing contests, Julienne. You need to pull up your math and science grades first. Those C's and D's will spoil your college transcript.'' A's in English and history didn't mean a whole lot to my mother. Those are not as ''marketable'' as the subjects I don't do so well in.

Still, it wouldn't hurt to give the contest a try, would it? My chances of winning weren't great, but I figured it was worth a try.

I got off the bus at the park, huddling down into my hooded jacket, and thinking that one of the good things about moving to Webber Falls lay just a couple of hundred feet away. Briar Grove Stables. It looked like just a bunch of white buildings, but it offered virtually all I'd ever wanted out of Real Life. Excitement. Romance. Horses.

Back in Portland, I could never do more than dream of riding. Until our very last year there, finances had been tight, and the sum total of my allowance wouldn't have rented a horse's left ear.

I walked faster along the crunchy gravel path. It seemed too dark to be only three-thirty. The sky was a menacing gray, and the late October wind bit at my nose and ears. My skin prickled against the cold. But I didn't mind at all. The thought of riding was making me feel alive again, after a long, dead day at school.

The sharp smell of hay and horses greeted me at the ring, where another one of the good things about Webber Falls was jumping his champion, Avenger, over the course. I leaned up against the white rail to watch Gregory Peloux, who was wearing only his tight, faded jeans and a T-shirt, despite the cold. His horse, Avenger, was black and sleek with a daring slash of white down his nose. Gregory sat straight and graceful, just the way he wanted me to look on a horse.

It wasn't easy having an instructor like Gregory Peloux. For one thing, it was very hard to concentrate on anything but him. For another, he couldn't be pleased and hardly ever smiled. When he did, everything lit up. His robin's-egg-blue eyes, coal-black hair, broad shoulders—everything about him—smiled. But usually only for Laura. His wife.

I tore myself away from the rail and headed for the office, a little white cabin at one end of the ring. In my dreams, Laura was never anywhere in sight. Gregory smiled for *me*. But out here in the irritatingly real world, I had to deal with Laura. She scheduled the lessons, rented out the horses, and took my money. Half my allowance went for one Tuesday afternoon lesson per week. Most of the rest, I spent on my regular Friday afternoon trail ride. That didn't leave much. But at least I got to ride.

My first shock of the afternoon came when I saw just which horse they expected me to ride that day. As Laura adjusted her bridle, the mare's strawberry roan coat glistened in the dim stable light. She pranced from hoof to hoof and tossed her head, snorting clouds of steam out into the cold.

Laura smiled, throwing back one of her blond braids. "Greg says you're ready for her, Julienne. And I'll bet you wouldn't pass her up."

"Oh, no," I breathed. "I wouldn't."

Who would? Mirage was one of the finest mounts at Briar Grove. Tall for a mare, she was half-Arabian—and feisty.

My heart was pounding wildly. On one hand, there was nothing in the world that would make me skip the chance to ride Mirage. On the other, I was nagged by a little voice that told me I was going to end up somewhere in Wyoming if I put so much as a foot in the stirrup.

"Well, she's ready to go," Laura urged, holding her for me.

"Oh. O.K. Thanks," I stammered.

It was now or never.

Now, I decided, and swung into the saddle. And that was the moment when I felt things changing over, like when you

6

switch channels on television. I was no longer in Webber Falls, Oregon. I was no longer a Frazier High junior, or a beginning rider, or even Audrey Kelsey's only daughter.

I was in *their* world, with Lady Eleanor and Lord Reynold, where things were exciting and romantic and wonderful. We were off. Mirage strained against me, nibbling at the bit and tossing her head. She flared her delicate nostrils and nervously sidestepped a little plastic bag half-filled with mud. But my doubts had vanished. I didn't have to worry about being able to handle her. In an automatic reflex, I had once again slipped away from Real Life.

Preparing myself with a deep, even breath, I turned Mirage's head to the side and pushed my heels down. She broke into a canter.

I smiled with confidence as her hooves fell in a smooth rhythm on the trail. Almost without thinking, I started to post, rising up and forward from the saddle on every other beat.

I hardly noticed that we were wandering off the horse trail and into the public park. There were big, thick-trunked oaks and slim pines every dozen feet or so, and rows of picnic tables close by. The eerie quiet was disturbed only by the steady rustle of Mirage's hooves through the fallen leaves. Seeing that we had the clearing all to ourselves, I broke her into a full gallop.

The wind sang past my ears and lifted my hair. This was worth every penny I had been handing over to Laura every week. I was flying, deep in my fantasy that Mirage, the most magnificent horse on earth, was winging me to the man I loved. He would be waiting there, at the next trail junction, to whisk me away to safety and serenity in a magical kingdom. We'd reign there, together . . .

I leaned forward to let the wind roll over me, and held the crop out to spur Mirage on faster.

It was at that moment, while galloping exactly the way Gregory would have wanted, that I felt something like a high-voltage electric shock. Because there actually was someone up ahead. A tall, male, and very real someone.

Chapter Two

The next few seconds passed very quickly. All I knew was that I was slipping downward, while Mirage was rearing upward. And there was a distinct, persistent barking somewhere nearby.

The most important thing, I remember thinking, was to hold on. So my legs were clamped around Mirage, and I leaned forward until my nose was buried in her thick red mane.

She calmed down. As she stopped galloping, her front hooves hit the ground with a force that made my joints ache. Gradually I became aware of the source of the constant barking. It was a dog, a very small one. And the tall, male, very real someone was struggling to hold onto it.

For a while I must have just sat there in the saddle, reining in a fidgety Mirage and staring at the someone holding the dog. I was stunned. Of all the boys in all of Webber Falls to find standing there waiting for me, just as I had imagined! Peter Garroway was nice. He had actually smiled at me a couple of times, and was one of the only boys at Frazier who had ever said so much as hi to me in the halls. Romantic heroes were supposed to swagger and smirk and keep their women in total, unsettled uncertainty. Peter, on the other hand, had always seemed solid as a rock and perfectly normal. His hair was just a medium color—between blond and brown. His eyes were just a medium color—bluish-green. He wasn't too skinny or too muscular. Nothing about him had been too anything.

Until that moment.

Suddenly, while staring down at him holding the dog, I began to notice things like the rich honey highlights in his hair, and how broad his shoulders were.

There he was, fondling a tiny, helpless dog and murmuring affectionately to it. It melted my heart.

"Sorry about that, Julienne." I could barely understand him, but I did hear my name, loud and clear. There was no doubt in my mind that he had said it. He actually knew my name. And we didn't even have any classes together!

I had absolutely no idea of what to say. All I knew was that he was standing right there in front of me, talking to me, in Real Life.

It was too much.

Without thinking, I dug my heels into Mirage's flanks and bounded away.

By Monday morning, I *still* felt like kicking myself. How could I have been so cowardly? The scene in the park couldn't have been staged more perfectly to meet Peter Garroway. I could have at least said hello, or said *something*.

It was no use. All I had done was run away.

"And why?" I asked the face in the bathroom mirror. (As usual, it was pale, almost creamy white. Only my cheeks were a bit rosier, and the band of freckles across my nose a shade darker, thanks to a hot shower.) Why couldn't I have said something before taking off?

I popped the toothbrush into my mouth and scrubbed furiously. Maybe if the TV set in my brain hadn't been stuck on Channel DREAM, I might have been able to react to Peter Garroway like a normal person would.

And the more I thought about Peter (something I had been doing most of the weekend), the more I realized that he had been there all along. Little hellos in the hallways, occasional passing grins, and then yesterday . . . I remembered the way he had looked at me. What color were his eyes? Aquamarine? Turquoise? I thought about his square jaw, with that Christopher Reeve dimple in the middle of it. He had known my name! It wasn't much to go on, but it was better than anything I'd had all year.

Pulling a wide-toothed comb from the roots of my hair down to the ends, I stared into the brown eyes in the mirror and let myself off the hook, I had made a mistake by running away from him. But it wasn't the end of the world. And maybe it wasn't such a terrible mistake. My quick exit had been dramatic, hadn't it? At least he wouldn't be likely to forget me.

And he had known my name!

The memory made me sail to my closet and pick out my current favorite outfit—the Cossack look.

Dressed and feeling daring, I headed for the kitchen. That was probably my first mistake of the day. My mother sat at the table with her tea, waiting to give me her customary once-over morning inspection.

11

"Morning, honey," she greeted, looking up from the paper. Her eyes swept in one glance from the black felt cap on my head to my magenta suede calf-high boots, not missing a stitch.

I took a deep breath, waiting for her to say something. Instead, she turned back to the paper. "There's sliced pineapple in the fridge."

"Thanks," I answered, with a small sigh of relief. The last thing I needed this morning was another "discussion." With the plate of pineapple and a bowl of granola, I sat down.

"There's a notice here about the exhibit," she said.

"Maura's?"

" 'Abstract expressionism by local artists Maura Higgins, Robert Nordstrom, and Rowena Tyson at the Village Gallery,' " she quoted. " 'Wine and cheese opening Saturday night.' "

"Good publicity," I said.

My mother shrugged. "It could be better. As their friend, I suppose I'm biased, but Maura and Bob and Rowena are not unknowns."

She took off her glasses and set them on the table. That let me see straight into her plan. It's amazing that she can accomplish anything in the business world with talkative eyes like hers. They're almond-shaped and slightly turned up at the edges, like mine, and fringed with the same thick, dark lashes she passed on to me. But hers are pale blue. You can see directly through them to whatever she's thinking.

Now she was about to comment on my outfit. I knew it.

She got up and put her cup in the sink. Everything about her seemed brisk and efficient. Just an inch taller and six pounds heavier than I, her figure is trim and petite. Nothing extra.

She dresses the part. I can't believe that there's anyone else in the world who owns more business suits. Today, it was the navy wool-silk blend, with a quiet print blouse. My mother seemed to do her best to look like an airline ticket clerk. You could probably have found at least seven hundred other women in the state of Oregon wearing the same thing that day.

She peered through the window over the sink, shaking her head. "It's supposed to drop down to forty this afternoon. Can you believe it? It looks so warm out there now. You should probably take your jacket."

"I'll be warm enough," I said.

"Hmm. I guess that's one practical thing about your outfit."

There, I knew it was coming.

She smiled to let me know she wasn't trying to give me a hard time. But it wasn't easy to keep from getting upset. Did I have to wear a navy blue suit, too?

I could tell she didn't want to be late for work. After giving me a quick peck, she grabbed her leather attaché case and headed for the door.

"Oh." She stopped midway. "Why don't you take some of that quiche for lunch?"

"Good idea," I said, trying to smile. I really didn't want to have any arguments this morning. There was so much to feel good about.

She smiled back, obviously pleased that we weren't parting on a sour note. For a second, I saw something I couldn't quite figure out in her eyes. Just the barest hint, maybe, of worry.

"Well, I'm off." She waved. "Love you."

13

"Love you, too, Mom." I don't think she heard. It wasn't something I said very often, or very loud.

As soon as she shut the door, I felt the room get a little bigger. Somehow, any space my mother and I occupied together always seemed too small. Our new townhouse was a real improvement over the little apartment we had rented in Portland, or even over the big old house we had lived in when my father was alive. But I couldn't help missing that house, and the way things had been back then. No matter how hard I tried, I couldn't help wishing sometimes for a "regular" kind of life, with a yard and a dog and a mother who would wave me off from the front porch with a lunch she had packed herself.

But I had to admit that moving to Webber Falls was an improvement. For one thing, my mother didn't lecture me half as much as she used to. When she worked as a secretary, she would come home acting about as motherly as a typewriter. Just about all she could talk about was how she wanted me to get a "marketable" education and not an art degree, like hers. She had let up some after her promotion to administrative assistant. And now that she was a manager of the Blackmon Electronics Northwest district office, she was relaxing even more. Being a manager wasn't as "thankless" as being a secretary, so I guess she felt much better about her life and the "plight of women," as she put it. The more established she got in her career, the less she bothered me about my life. Up to a point.

I jumped up and ran to my room. I was absolutely not going to get caught up in all those old feelings again. There were other things to think about today. Peter Garroway, for instance. First, I decided that I had definitely made some sort of impression on him. Then, just as quickly, I decided that he had probably forgotten all about me. But maybe just for this one day, I could come down out of the clouds. Because if I had managed to get Peter's attention once, I was bound and determined I could get it again.

Chapter Three

I discovered one thing right away. Peter hadn't forgotten me.

I saw him about five minutes after I got to school, on my way to chemistry. The halls were crammed with people making last-minute dashes for their classes. For some reason, everyone seemed to be running late this morning. Except Peter. He was the picture of calm as he walked along in his own lane of traffic, out of everyone's way.

At first I was disappointed. According to the law of averages, I probably wouldn't see him again that day. This was my only chance, and I was too rushed to take advantage of it. Out of the corner of my eye, I saw him turn off toward Room 142. Room 142, first-period junior English, was right next door to Room 144, which just happened to be *my* first-period chemistry.

All semester long, Peter had been in the class next door to mine, and I hadn't even noticed!

Just before the stream of traffic carried me off, I pushed my way toward the door. Then I saw him and his smile.

He hadn't gone in to class. He was just standing there, with one hand on the doorknob, watching me. I froze, as if all of Frazier High School had just evaporated.

"Hello, again," he said. That was all. But his smile wrapped itself around my heart and said half a million things, including the fact that he hadn't forgotten me.

Before I could crumple into a swooning heap, he pushed through the doorway and disappeared.

So much for my chemistry class and any concentration I might have applied to it. As Ms. Caulfield droned on, I barely heard. The only type of chemistry I had any mind for was the kind that drew Peter and me together.

Together, I said to myself. No boy in the entire school had ever so much as looked my way before, as far as I knew. The only date I'd ever had was an arranged, practically forced, trip to the movies with another one of my mother's friends' offspring, Tim Sammels. *Dull, dull, dull* had been the word for him. Neither of us had seen the need for a repeat performance.

But now there was Peter. A dozen images flashed before my eyes. Peter and me, hand in hand on a rocky, windswept beach. Peter and me, sipping something hot and spicy before a crackling wood fire. Peter and me, laughing at a bear in the zoo.

I automatically copied the formulas Ms. Caulfield was writing on the board. But my mind was someplace else. It focused on a face, the one I had seen just moments before. A square-jawed, dimple-chinned face with blue-green eyes. I could drown in those eyes. The memory of his smile carried me on a soft, warm cloud until lunch.

Blair was alone at our table near the water fountain.

"Hi there," she said as I sat down. "Have a good weekend?"

Today, for the first time, I didn't have to look at her twice to make sure she wasn't teasing me. My weekends were nothing compared to hers. But today, I didn't feel suspicious. Today, if Blair felt like being friendly, well—great. I wasn't going to question her motives.

"Pretty good," I answered.

"Well, mine was on the dull side. Would you believe my dear mother made me clean out the basement?" She shook her head and rolled her dark eyes. "It was disgusting!"

I had to laugh. "Why? What was down there?"

"Oh, everything! Rusty golf clubs, socks, moldy old frames and canvases that she stuck down there and forgot about. You'd never know she had a whole studio to herself upstairs, for all the art supplies I found. What a waste!"

"Mothers are a mystery to me, too," I sympathized, stepping willingly into a subject I normally stayed away from. Most of the problem between Blair and me was that we knew too much about each other through our mothers, who wanted desperately for us to get along. But today I was brave.

"Anyway," she was saying, "how's it going in Hoff's trig class for you?"

It was a perfectly reasonable question, I told myself. She had Hoff second period.

"Okay, I guess. Same as usual."

"For a class as easy as his is supposed to be, a lot of people sure did get bruised on that last test."

"Hmm," I mumbled, feeling myself tense up. Just how much about me and my math grades had my mother confided to Blair's?

Her attention suddenly focused on something just beyond my left shoulder. Thinking it must be Stephen, I turned around to greet him. But what I saw instead was a group of three boys at the drinking fountain. They were clowning around, rowdily nudging each other out of the way to be first in line. One of them was Andy Hanes, a burly, six-foot-four, star football player, who had a clear advantage over the other two. Another was Matt Forster, who was short and slim and happened to be the most brilliant person in my math class. I would have just gone back to my lunch and ignored them, if it hadn't been for one thing. The third guy horsing around was Peter Garroway.

That kept my eyes riveted.

By the time they had finished drinking, I was prepared. I was ready to dazzle him with my smile. The same kind he had given me this morning. This time, I was going to let him see that I remembered him, too.

It would have been perfect. My smile was casual and friendly. But he looked right through me. Andy was on one side of him. Matt Forster was on the other. They all three looked straight at me and my charming smile, and none of them saw me. They just turned away and kept walking.

I was still invisible.

Chapter Four

Stuck in Mr. Hoff's math class last period, I pretended to take a quiz. There was no way that I could even attempt to answer more than three of the questions. They made no sense to me. It was only a quiz, anyway. I'd be better prepared for the exam next week, by which time I'd have gotten over Peter Garroway.

The creep.

How dare he smile at me the way he had this morning, then completely ignore me just a few hours later!

After another halfhearted attempt to solve the quiz problems, I put them aside in favor of the blank worksheet Mr. Hoff had given us for scratch paper.

I began to write.

Long ago, he cradled her like the most fragile of treasures.

But it was all in the past, Rebecca realized with a jolt. Reed was gone from her life now.

"Five more minutes," Mr. Hoff warned.

I kept writing.

Rebecca padded across her boudoir to her washbasin. Reflected in the mirror was a strange face, one she would never grow accustomed to. It seemed to have aged in the two years since Reed's sudden departure.

"All right. Time's up. Hand in the quizzes, please."

The bell rang. I folded the worksheet carefully into my notebook, and tugged on my jacket, still envisioning Rebecca. The bustle and hubbub of Frazier High at three-fifteen faded into a dim blur. There was only Rebecca and her pain.

After dressing, Rebecca descended the marble staircase of the great manse of which she was now mistress.

Blair waved to me happily as we passed in the hall. She was walking hand in hand with Stephen.

I pressed on toward my locker.

The large, marble-floored foyer glittered brightly, having been freshly cleaned and polished the previous day at Rebecca's orders. Trevor Ridge House must be perfect tonight.

Absently, I turned the knob on my lock and heard the combination click into place. The rise and fall of conversations and the slam of metal doors faded away. It was not my locker door I threw open, but a set of glass-paneled French doors that opened onto the broad, scenic veranda overlooking Trevor Ridge.

Rebecca closed her eyes to savor the scents of morning, then opened them to gaze over the gentle hills of the estate.

Half my mind decided to take home my three-ring binder, my biology, history, and grammar books, then instructed my hands to put them into the tote bag I held. The remaining half lingered with Rebecca.

She pulled the delicately embroidered shawl closer about her shoulders, and felt a little shiver up her spine. It must be the dream, Rebecca thought. That cruelly real dream she'd had of Reed just before waking. He had been there, as warm as life, holding her, comforting her, just as he had before . . . But she couldn't let herself fall into misery over Reed again. She had already gone over and over the memories of their brief, sweet time together, struggling for a clue as to what had driven him away.

Rebecca shuddered again, this time in revulsion. How could she have loved such an unscrupulous wolf?

I shut my locker door with a bang. Unscrupulous wolf. All men were alike.

She brought the French doors to a rattling close against the chilled breeze. This was a day for joy, for celebration. Finally it was time to emerge into a world full of dancing and gaiety and dozens of worthy suitors.

Not another thought of him today, she promised herself. He was all in the past.

Slinging the tote bag over my shoulder, I turned away and began a resolute march down the hall. Yes, he was all in the past.

She turned to reposition one of the potted violets in the solarium. It was at that moment, with her head bent over the delicate blossoms, that she heard the footsteps—and the voice.

She was paralyzed.

"Julienne?"

I whirled around.

She dropped the bowl of violets. It shattered into a thousand pieces.

Chapter Five

Peter had already picked up my book bag and handed it to me. I barely had time to shake myself back into reality.

"Here you go. Sorry I startled you again."

I wasn't startled. I was mesmerized. He was back, and smiling again. His eyes were lighting up the whole gloomy hallway. I was afraid I had dreamed him up.

"I thought—well, I was hoping you might like to come with me to The Snax for a Coke or something, just to make up for having caused you all that trouble in the park the other day. You have time today?"

If the building had suddenly caught on fire, I couldn't have felt more panicked. It was like the moment before deciding to ride Mirage. A date with Peter? Today? After almost two semesters of hardly ever even *talking* to boys?

Now or never, I told myself.

"No," I muttered. "I have to go home today. Sorry."

I could handle Mirage. I could not handle Peter Garroway.

He narrowed his eyes to stare at me. Good. Maybe he would get mad and go away.

"How about if I walk with you, then?" he said suddenly.

I swallowed. Why was he being so persistent? Why wouldn't he just let me go back to my dreams?

"Just up to the corner. How about that? I promise I won't make you late." He was smiling.

And that was my undoing, because that smile of his was contagious. My lips caught a little of it and smiled back. My whole body was operating on its own. *To heck with you,* it seemed to be telling my brain. *To heck with your daydreams and your fear of getting hurt. I'm going to walk with Peter Garroway.*

"Well," he was saying as we headed down the sidewalk, "I know how it is when you have to get right home after school. See, my parents run this business—they make up programs and games and stuff for small computers, then mail them out. That means that us kids, or the ones who are left, anyway—my sister and I—are drafted into all kinds of odd jobs. And sometimes I take care of people's pets when they're on vacation or something. So that means I have to rush home sometimes, too." He was still smiling.

I didn't know what *my* face was doing. I didn't really want to know. What I wanted was a brain that would think fast enough to give me something to *say.*

"Oh," was all it provided.

"Well," Peter said quickly. "I guess this is the corner. See ya."

Just like that, before I could even wave, he turned and dashed away.

(*Footsteps echo offstage. Music rises*)
I scratched out the entire line and started over.

It was awful. How could I expect to get the contest judges to read my entry if the first line was so awful?

I grabbed up the sheet of paper and crumpled it into a hard little ball. It landed in the metal waste can with a thunk. Just for good measure, I gave the can a solid kick.

It was a better kick than I had planned on.

"Julienne? You O.K. in there?" my mother shouted up from the den.

"I'm fine," I yelled back, hoping she wouldn't decide to investigate further.

It was too late. I heard her climbing the stairs.

"What's going on, honey? You've been banging around in there all evening. Can I come in?" she asked, knocking softly.

"Sure."

I was frowning over my math book by the time she opened the door.

Her face filled with sympathy when she saw me. "Is it that bad?"

"Yeah, I guess it is that bad," I answered, not lying. Nothing was going well tonight. I couldn't concentrate on writing or math or anything but the big, fat mistake I had made by freezing Peter out that afternoon. I had ruined everything.

"Listen, honey," my mother began, sitting on the edge of my desk so that the sleeves of her midnight blue silk kimono draped over a stack of books. It was the one beautiful, frivolous article of clothing she owned, and I had given it to her. "I know how hard math can be. I wasn't so good at it, either, until I took that remedial course last summer. But it's so important . . ." Her voice trailed off on a pleading note.

I knew what was coming, and groaned inwardly. Another lecture. All I needed now. She continued, gaining momentum.

"Until just last year, honey, you were making spectacular

grades across the board. You can do math as easily as anything else. Maybe you just need to give it a little more effort.'' She smiled supportively.

I tried not to glare at her. "It's a lot harder than my other subjects, Mother.''

"Oh, Julienne,'' she consoled. "I know how frustrating it is. It's easy to get the idea that no matter how much you study, it won't help. As we've discussed before, a lot of girls and women have 'math anxiety' because of the way society sometimes treats math and even science as somehow more 'masculine' subjects. But that's just baloney. You can't let that propaganda get to you.''

"Mother, I'm not brainwashed,'' I insisted, rolling my eyes.

"That's not what I'm trying to say, Julienne.''

By the look in her eyes, I could tell that was *exactly* what she was trying to say.

"I just want to make sure you don't give up. It's really important to learn the basics in this trigonometry class. It will make classes much easier for you later, in college. What *I* did was convince myself that all I needed was an art degree, and that somehow I'd be able to support myself by selling those paintings I thought were so great.'' She waved a hand toward the one I had over my desk, then sighed wearily.

"I know you've heard this all before. But you've got to develop the skills to survive out there, honey.''

"I know how to write.''

She smiled. "I know you do, sweetheart. It's something to be proud of. But it's also hard to sell. There's an awful lot of competition in that field. You need to develop more market-able talents.''

Marketable. I thought I'd scream if I heard that word one more time.

"Well, enough said. I've got to get back to my paperwork.

And you to yours. Just remember, Julienne, I'm confident you can accomplish whatever you set your mind to, including this." She tapped her finger on a set of unsolved equations. "You can do it."

With that, she gave me a quick hug and left the room.

She was right about one thing. Math and science really weren't that much harder for me than anything else. But I just couldn't concentrate on them. Other subjects, like English and history, were more interesting. Did that have to mean that I was brainwashed?

I blinked my eyes hard, amazed to find them stinging with unshed tears. Being angry with my mother never made me cry. It was only when she was understanding that I wanted to bawl.

A good hot bubble bath was what I needed.

While the tub filled, I gathered up an armful of towels and bath oils. I needed all the help I could get. It started to work almost as soon as I sunk into the lavender-scented, steamy suds.

She watched him stride toward her. A tall, rugged man whose gentleness she alone knew. His gold-brown hair, the green-blue of his eyes . . .

No matter how I tried, all I could see was Peter when I searched for an image of the hero. And he was always wearing a mocking, teasing sort of smile meant to show me just how ridiculous I was being.

I shook my head. I had to get Peter out of my thoughts, once and for all. How could anything develop between us now, after the way I had acted today? And why on earth had he ignored my smile in the cafeteria, then looked for me later?

I tried to relax and think back to all my heroines. What would they do? Would any of them shrug and give up? Would Lavinia be so timid? Or Thomasa or Melanie or Rebecca?

Once they knew they wanted a man, they went after him, didn't they?

I jumped up and rinsed off with a cold stinging spray. After toweling dry, I practically showered with a bottle of *Je Reviens,* and thought about what that name meant in French. It seemed perfectly appropriate, and prophetic.

I will return, I chanted dreamily. *I will return.*

Chapter Six

With that phrase in mind, I walked into the cafeteria the next day, looking for Peter. The hardest part of putting my plan into action, I told myself, would be to find him. But after I did, I realized that the worst was yet to come. Because there he was, with Andy Hanes and Matt Forster at a table by the windows. A table that I had no logical reason to walk casually by.

"Julienne! Are you rooted to the spot? I've been *trying* to get your attention."

It was Blair, on Stephen's arm. They were both staring at me as though I were a large tree in the middle of the cafeteria.

Smiling, she said, "I just wanted to tell you that when you're tired of standing there, you should come over and sit with us at Cathleen and Linda's table."

Cathleen and Linda's table! It was just a row away and two tables down from Peter's!

"Oh, thanks. I'll be right there."

They nodded and walked on, giving me a chance to take a deep breath and prepare. All I had to do was smile. What was there to worry about? I remembered the last time I had tried smiling at Peter. *That* was what I had to worry about—being invisible. What if I just stood there, smiling like an idiot, and he didn't notice?

I'll make him notice, I told myself. Wouldn't Lady Eleanor be noticed? Or Rebecca? How could I let them down?

Mentally, I switched channels. For just this once more, I promised, I would pretend that I wasn't really me, and that this wasn't really the grimy old Frazier High cafeteria. My heroines would see me through.

Walking down the aisle, I felt Lady Eleanor's silky mass of blond hair covering my shoulders and Rebecca's brocade cape swirling gracefully about my feet. At the sixth table down, I slowed my pace and forced my head to turn.

He noticed. For the briefest of seconds, I thought he smiled back.

Before the old panic could rise up again, I walked on.

For the next couple of hours, all I could think of was that I had done it—I hadn't backed out. Did it really matter that I had to go back to pretending, just for a few measly seconds? It wasn't until the end of the day, when I was headed for my locker, that I began to worry about whether or not my plan had worked. I hadn't seen Peter since lunch. What could he possibly think of a girl who was as unpredictable as me?

Just steps away from my locker, I realized that I was about to find out. A cold prickle went up my spine. There was no chance for escape.

"Hi," he said, as he started walking along beside me. It was a casual, matter-of-fact greeting, as if we'd known each other for years. When we got to my locker, I opened it, and Peter held the door open for me and smiled. "How about if I walk you home today?"

"Today?" was all that came out of my mouth.

"If you're not busy," he answered.

Quickly, before I could panic, I nodded yes.

Looking back, I've often thought that I must have been in some sort of trance during those early moments with Peter. It was as if my brain had taken a back-door exit from my body. But somehow, I made it out to the street.

"Which way?" he asked.

I motioned westward. Walking beside him, I wondered if it were possible for my temperature to have risen several degrees in the last few seconds. Just having Peter there, with the dimpled cleft in his chin and his silky, thick brown eyebrows, was enough to make me dizzy.

Why couldn't I naturally be like one of the heroines in the novels I knew by heart? Confident, poised, witty?

"I suppose I should let you know, Julienne, that I . . ." He cleared his throat. "I have a reason for wanting to walk with you."

He was looking straight at me.

"I caused you a lot of trouble that day in the park, making your horse go wild and everything. I got the feeling yesterday that maybe you were still sore at me over it."

He might as well have dropped a piano on me.

"Sore?" I repeated in a half-whisper.

"Well, yeah. I thought . . . you know. Maybe you were upset."

I didn't want to do it. I wanted to answer Peter in my own voice, as *me*, Julienne Kelsey. But the channel changed almost automatically this time, as panic choked me up.

It began with a toss of my head.

31

"Upset?" I asked. "Me?" My laugh—no, Lady Eleanor's laugh—was a wind chime. "Not at all."

I looked up at him sideways, through *her* sparkling emerald eyes. "Whatever gave you that idea? You didn't cause me any trouble at all, Peter. That horse is just too excitable. She spooks at everything."

"She does?"

"Why, yes," I continued. "As a matter of fact, it was good for me. It made the ride more . . . interesting." I drawled out the last word.

His eyes widened again. "Really?" he asked, as if he couldn't believe it.

I knew he must be in shock over the fact that I was actually making conversation, but I tried not to think about it. If I started thinking about making conversation, it would never work. What I had to do was smile.

"Well, I'm glad you don't hate me," Peter said, with a grin. His pace had slowed. "And you know what? Up there on that horse, you looked like you had no doubts at all about what to do. If it had been me . . ." He shook his head. "Horses don't like me too much."

I lowered my eyes and grabbed a deep breath. What I was about to say took every ounce of courage I had. "But you look like you could handle just about anything, Peter."

It came out so softly that I was sure he hadn't heard. All he did was cough a little and sort of straighten his shoulders. Then he turned to look at me. And that very nearly made me fall apart, because it reminded me of the simple fact that Peter was real.

Peter as a noble knight, or a lusty pirate, or a colonial adventurer was a Peter I could handle. But Peter as Peter was another story altogether. And sooner or later, I was going to have to come to terms with it. I decided that sooner or later was going to have to be now. All I had to do was relax and be myself, right? No fantasies. This was Real Life.

Fortunately, Peter started talking enough for both of us.

"I live just a couple of blocks up that way, on the street where some college students made that movie in the old house everyone says is haunted."

"Oh, that's nice," I said, then felt like wiring my jaw shut. Nothing I said sounded right.

"Yeah, it was really wild to have them running around with cameras and lights and everything. Oh, and speaking of movies," he continued. "My friends and I saw this one flick, *Fly by Night*. It was kind of a sci-fi thriller type of thing, but not real spooky or gross. Do you like movies like that?"

I had to grit my teeth to keep from exclaiming (in Rebecca's voice), "Oh, absolutely, Peter!" All I let myself do was nod.

"They've got this sequel out now, *Fly by Day*, and I've heard it's pretty good. Are you interested? Maybe for this Saturday night?"

I didn't fly into a fantasy. Somehow, I managed to accept the invitation without any pretending. Even on my front doorstep, when he gave my shoulder a soft squeeze, I just smiled. The fact that I was near hysteria didn't break down my resolve to be me, Julienne, and not a Channel DREAM heroine.

Chapter Seven

After shutting the door behind me and flying upstairs to my room, I was still trembling.

"Glad we had a chance to talk, Julienne," Peter had said. "I'll be in touch about the movie...I'll look for you at school."

None of it had been in a book or a dream. It had really happened.

Just when I was about to drop my tote bag and collapse, I remembered that it was Tuesday. Gregory Peloux day. Peter had just made me forget all about a whole hour's worth of riding with Gregory Peloux.

I dialed the number at the stables and told Laura I was too sick to ride.

"No problem," she sympathized. "Get better."

I really did feel sick. Cold sweat, numbness, blurred vision, queasy stomach. I pulled off my dress and got under the covers. Had I really accepted a Saturday night date? And had I really spent a good half hour actually talking with Peter Garroway?

He had asked me out. Saturday, just four days away, I was going to a movie with him.

I closed my eyes and let my heart do its gymnastic routine. It did somersaults when I pictured myself getting into Peter's car, getting out of Peter's car, walking into the theater, finding seats, sitting next to him. I felt his arm slip over my shoulders. His fingers, gentle and warm, on my arm. Soft breath in my hair. His knee against mine. I sighed.

Two-and-a-half hours later, I awoke to the sound of my mother calling up from the kitchen.

"Julienne, hon. You home?"

I sat up.

"Yes," I yelled back groggily.

"Good! I have something to show you." I heard her take the stairs two at a time.

Within seconds, she was standing in my doorway behind the most hideous blue dress I had ever seen.

"What do you think?" she asked, still holding it up.

"About what?"

"For Saturday night. Would you like to try it on?" She was peeking out at me.

"That? But I couldn't—" I was about to thank her politely and go back to dreaming. Then, it occurred to me that maybe I *was* dreaming. My mother couldn't possibly know about Peter, or about Saturday night.

She burst into her soft, dove's-coo laughter. "I guess our tastes don't match very well, do they? No matter. It can go back. I just had such a terrific day at work that I felt like splurging on this for you for Maura's exhibit opening, in case you liked it." She moved closer. "Why are you so pale, honey?"

Saturday night was why I was so pale. How could I have forgotten? There was Peter, and there was my mother's best friend's big art show party, which I had promised to attend.

"You're not running a fever, are you?" Mother sat down on the bed and pressed her hand to my forehead. "Nope, you feel fresh as a daisy. Have you been taking your iron tablets?"

"Faithfully," I mumbled.

"Good." She gave me a little hug. "This isn't the best week to come down with something, you know. Saturday night will mark the opening of the first serious art show in Webber Falls history, if anyone cares." She was laughing again.

"I know, Mom, but—"

"And besides that, I'm anxious to show you off to all my old art department buddies who will be there. Maura, of course, is counting on you to bring her good luck, superstitious as she is, and—"

"Mom."

"Yes, honey?"

"I . . ."

She was smiling so blissfully that I couldn't say another word.

My life would have remained a complete mess if it hadn't been for Blair, who unintentionally came to my rescue.

We sat at lunch the day after my mother's surprise. I was too depressed to pay much attention to Blair's talk about the new photography club. Politely, I acknowledged her cheerful chatter with an occasional nod. The rest of the time, I brooded.

So much was going through my head that I almost didn't notice when Stephen sat down. And I almost didn't hear Blair's question.

"Do you think this monster is going to be a total embarrassment to us at the opening on Saturday night, Julienne?"

My eyes flew up to see her poking at poor Stephen. He cringed, then bared his teeth in a Dracula impersonation.

"You're going?" I demanded urgently.

"Vy, uff course," Stephen leered.

Blair rolled her eyes in disgust, but I felt like kissing him, and her.

Why hadn't I thought of it before? It was the answer to everything. Asking Peter to the show would keep everyone happy. Maybe he would even enjoy it. Especially if Blair was bringing Stephen. Then Peter wouldn't feel *too* out of place. And with Maura and all the other eccentrics there, he certainly wouldn't be bored.

The weight of a Steinway grand had just been lifted off my shoulders. My problems were solved. Almost.

Now, all I had to do was talk to Peter.

Chapter Eight

Talk to Peter. That was all I had to do. It was enough to make me queasy all afternoon. I was half-praying and half-dreading that I would see him in the halls. I had let him know about my mistake right away. Of course, that didn't mean I was really prepared to talk to him. Even after the whole day had passed without my seeing him, I wasn't prepared.

In front of the mirror the next morning, I worked out my strategy. I would wait for him in front of Room 142 before first period. He would step aside with me and discuss the problem, accept my invitation, and that would be that. I wanted to believe it would be easy. After arranging a dramatically trailing scarf around my neck, I grabbed up my books and flew off to school.

He was late. Ms. Caulfield walked past me into the classroom and gave me a puzzled frown as she shut the door. In another minute, I would be late, too.

That was when he finally appeared.

"Julienne," he said, walking right up to me. He was beaming. "Hi!"

"Hi!" I answered, in exactly the same tone of voice, trying to remember what it was I was doing there. The only thing I could think of was the way he was looking at me. I couldn't look away from his eyes.

"We're late, you know," he grinned.

"Yes," I mumbled, pulling myself together. "I wanted to . . . talk."

"Oh," he said, then glanced at his watch.

"Maybe we should meet later," I offered.

"Oh, sure," he agreed. "I won't really have much time after first period. And I have to go home for lunch. How about walking home after school again? Should we meet at your locker?"

"Number 5672," was all I could say.

"I remember."

He did?

"See you after school, then," he said, giving me another one of those fantastic smiles.

His smile was still with me when the end-of-school bell rang. Moments later, I spotted him from all the way down the hall, waiting for me at number 5672. For a split second, I considered running in the opposite direction. But I knew that wasn't what I really wanted to do.

Not until we had gotten outside did I even begin my speech. He had his hands stuffed into the pockets of his blue parka. His apple-cider gold hair was being tossed all over in the wind. I would have been happy just to walk beside him, watching him and listening to his description of boredom in his third-period class with Mr. Hoff.

Instead, I had to talk to him. I knew I did. But no particular set of words seemed right.

"You have him, too, don't you?" Peter was asking.

"Him?" I repeated. "Who—" I had to rattle myself back into the conversation. "Oh, Hoff. He's so easy to forget, you know." *Dumb remark*, I thought. *He'll know I wasn't paying attention*.

But Peter laughed and I knew everything was all right. "True. My friend Matt has him last period. Aren't you in there?"

"Yes. What a way to end the day." Had Peter researched my schedule? And was I actually talking to him without pretending? I had to smile. It was all working out, right here on planet Earth.

But then we turned onto Vaquero Street, and I realized that after another couple of blocks we would be home. I gathered my thoughts.

Somehow, over the next block, I managed to communicate two things to Peter. One was how much I looked forward to Saturday night. He seemed pleased, and started to ask if I really didn't mind seeing *Fly by Day*, which he explained was really not a gore film but a science fiction classic. Before he could get much further, I interrupted with the second item. The problem. That was when things got a little harder.

All my confidence withered. Being face to face with Peter was so different from my imaginary conversations with him. But I had to go through with it.

"I'm afraid I've made a mistake," I finally said. "Saturday night . . ."

His slight frown jarred me. I began again. "Saturday night, Peter . . . there's a problem." I cleared my throat. "You see, my mother's friends are putting on an art show at the Village Gallery in town. I had forgotten all about it when you asked me out Tuesday." I paused to catch my breath. "And you see,

40

I can't miss it, Peter. It means so much to my mother. She's really counting on me.''

The blue in his eyes had gone ink-dark. He kept them focused on me, and seemed about to say something.

I spoke first. "I was wondering—"

But he interrupted before I could finish. "We could always go another night."

"Another . . . ?" I was thrilled. He wasn't angry. He was even willing to postpone the date. "Oh, sure. Another night. Good. But—"

"It doesn't have to be this week," he added. "Next weekend would be O.K."

He sounded happy, almost as if he had been hoping that he wouldn't have to go out with me *this* weekend. Maybe there was something else he wanted to do or someone else he wanted to see. Maybe I shouldn't even bother him with the show. But how could I back down now, after having made it this far?

"Next Saturday. All right," I answered. "But there's still the question of . . . whether or not you'd be interested in coming to the art show with me. I know it must sound terribly dull, but really, I think—"

"An art show?"

I thought he was going to laugh. He just smiled.

"Sure. I'd like that."

We stopped in front of the house.

"Should I come over to your house, then, Saturday night?" he asked.

"Oh. Yes. That sounds great. My mother's going, too. But she'll be riding with someone else."

He didn't even flinch.

"Seven o'clock?" I asked.

Peter nodded. "Seven o'clock." The shadows of a huge, broad-leafed tree dappled over him. "Saturday."

"Saturday," I repeated, smiling dumbly.

He kicked some stray gravel off the cobblestone path, then looked over his shoulder at the house.

"Well, I've got to go on in now. It's my afternoon to stuff envelopes."

"I see," I said, blind to everything but his eyes.

" 'Bye," Peter waved, and started up the path.

"Goodbye."

I turned back toward the sidewalk. Suddenly two things occurred to me. One was that I was on Vaquero Street at Peter's house, blocks away from my own.

The other was that we had just walked *him* home.

Chapter Nine

Peter and I arrived at the Village Gallery at a little after eight. All three tiny rooms were crowded with artists and with people in fancy clothes who had come to look at their work. Surprisingly, I was not nervous. In fact, for the first time in the short history of our "romance," I did not even consider acting like Melanie McNaughton or Dorinda Douglas or any other romantic heroine I had read about. Ever since Peter had shown up on my doorstep, I had stopped worrying.

That may have had something to do with the way he looked in a sports jacket and slacks. I was so busy thinking about how terrific he looked that I didn't have time to worry about myself. And Mother (who had been flattered by my asking to bring a friend to her old pals' art show) liked him. I could see it in her eyes.

The most wonderful thing was the plain fact that Peter was

there. He hadn't stood me up, and he wasn't yawning or scowling.

He turned to me with a whisper as we took off our coats in the gallery. "Do you actually *know* all these people?"

"Not all of them." I glanced around. "But a lot."

I was in a delicious daze. I remember chattering on and on about abstract art, in answer to all his questions, before Maura Higgins and my mother took us on a personal tour. Later we met up with Blair and Stephen, and decided to join them at the Dragon Palace Cafe two blocks away.

"Fortune cookies!" Blair cried as the waiter brought out a plate of them after the meal. She leaned forward in her chair, widening her eyes. "I'm nuts about fortune cookies. They are mysterious and sneaky. They—"

"Taste good," Stephen finished for her, popping a piece of one into her mouth.

After settling the bill, we stepped out into the coldest, clearest night we'd had all fall. The sky was full of stars. A light breeze carried the smell of snow and pine forest down from the mountains. We were all quiet.

Finally, Blair spoke up. "We'd better get going. Stephen can only take so much fresh air. He breaks out in hives at just the mention of outdoors."

"What a pair," Peter said as we watched them leave.

And it was at that moment, when I was completely off guard, that he slipped his hand into mine. His thumb brushed my palm ever so lightly, then closed in a warm clasp. Every square inch from my toes to my fingertips was alive and tingling with pleasure. But I couldn't believe it was happening. A boy, *this* boy (Peter!), was holding my hand. And I wasn't fainting away. I was even able to speak.

"It's beautiful out here."

"Yeah." His voice was husky. He cleared his throat and looked at me. I was afraid to look back. "Are you too cold to—" He broke off suddenly. "I mean, I know it's pretty chilly, but it's so nice out . . . Would you like to walk up to the fountains, maybe, before we head back to the car?"

I followed his gaze down the sidewalk, marveling that his hand could feel so enormous around mine. "I'm not cold at all," I mumbled.

We fell into step together, hand in hand on McDougall Avenue. It was suddenly the most beautiful street in the world.

Peter was staring up at the sky. "That's Orion," he said, pointing at a cluster of stars. "The Archer."

"Do you know the constellations?" I asked, trying to keep my voice even.

"Not that many. There are just a few I remember. These friends of mine and I used to be big astronomy freaks. We had star charts and predawn telescope meetings and all kinds of things. We were really into it."

"And now?"

"Oh, it's mostly Matt—um, Matt Forster. He still keeps up with it. But our common hobby these days is Conquest."

"What?"

"Oh. It's a game. You have a board with a map of this fantasy world, and little tokens representing armies and weapons, and cards to tell you whose side you're on. I know it sounds like kid stuff, but it's really challenging. Besides, we've been playing for a long time. It's kind of a tradition."

Actually, I was thinking about how lucky he was to have such good friends. And wondering whether he had told them about me. But I forced myself to concentrate on the game he was talking about. "What kind of fantasy world is it? I mean, past, or future, or—"

"It could be either, I guess. Just depends on what the players want."

Hmm. Fantasy. Maybe Peter and I had a lot in common.

All too soon, we stepped onto a cobblestone path that snaked around the Town Square fountains. We wandered there, watching the play of light and water from all angles.

Suddenly, the water rose in a lacy curtain, shielding us from the street. Only one small corner of the pond was still. And I saw the reflection of another constellation there.

"Look at those stars," I said, pointing. "Do you recognize them?"

Peter's reflection appeared beside the cluster.

"Maybe," he said.

And then, carefully, he kissed my hair. Just brushing my cheek, his breath was as warm as June. I stared into the water as he drew nearer.

"It's the Winged Horse, Pegasus."

"It is?" My voice was barely a whisper.

"It is."

Slowly, I turned toward him, and there, directly under the star-speckled flying horse, Peter Garroway kissed me.

Chapter Ten

I took my hands away from the typewriter and rested my chin on them. It was done. Twenty-five pages worth of mystery, suspense, and above all, romance. I called it *Hope for Love*. The manuscript was neatly typed and ready for the KWEB contest judges. At least, it was as ready as I could ever make it. I had been over and over it so many times that I could almost recite it by heart. And I just *had* to get back to schoolwork.

That minor detail was the only thing troubling me. Everything else about my life had been wonderful for the past two weeks. Ever since the night of the show opening, Peter and I had spent our time together at the movies, walking home, or over Cokes with Blair and Stephen. We'd had dinner at his house and at mine. I had never suspected that Real Life love could be so easy.

I shut my eyes and let my thoughts drift back to that

Saturday night exactly sixteen days before Peter's hands on my shoulders had been so light and gentle that I had felt cocooned in warm silk. When his lips touched mine, it was like nothing I had ever felt before. Perfect.

Now, sitting at my desk, I realized that I had never been so comfortable with anyone. Peter hadn't laughed at the dozens of romance novels crowding the bookshelves when he came for dinner one evening, or even at my suggestion that some of them could be made into films as successful as *Fly by Day* or *Star Wars*.

I looked at the stack of pages beside the typewriter. What kind of radio show would they make? My mother and I had been listening faithfully to the Theater Hour ever since we had come to Webber Falls. Other than that, what did I know about radio drama?

Waiting for the contest results would make the next four weeks last forever. I'd had to snatch every spare moment to work on my entry. And now it was time to send it out—to let it go.

"Julienne." My mother's voice was at the door. "May I speak with you for a moment?"

I shook myself into the present and ripped page twenty-five out of the typewriter. "Sure," I answered, stuffing the manuscript into a drawer.

She wore her blue kimono and a worried frown. "May I sit here?"

I nodded. As she picked stray clothes and other objects off my old armchair, I noticed the six-inch-square, pink slip of paper she held. It was not a bill, or a telegram, or a letter from her great-aunt Elsa. It was from Frazier High.

"You know, Julienne, I've never done this before," she began. "Although these come addressed to me, I've always let you open them yourself and show them to me voluntarily. It's *your* life and *your* career that will be affected."

I swallowed. "Are they that bad?"

She handed the computer printout to me.

"No, honey," she said as my eyes scanned it. "On the whole, they're not. In fact, I'm quite proud of you. You've never dipped below an A in English or history, and that B-plus in social studies is certainly nothing to complain about. But that's just it. Why is chemistry giving you so much trouble? And a D in trigonometry? What's happening? Until this year, it was A's all the way across."

I didn't look up. "It's harder this year."

My mother sighed. "Oh, Julienne. We've been over this so many times. How much harder can it be? I can't help thinking that—"

"Mother, why can't you just accept the fact that I'm not good in some subjects? Neither were you."

"Honey, listen. Don't ever forget how hard it's been for me trying to establish a career. Until last year, I was very poorly compensated for my work. If I'd had more technical skills, more *marketable* skills like a background in computer science or medical training—"

She saw me shudder.

"O.K." Her eyes leveled on mine. "Assuming that you're not caught up in myths about what you should and shouldn't be good at. Assuming that it *is* harder for you this year, then, you know, there are plenty of good tutors here, through the university."

"I don't want one."

She pounced. "Ah-hah! My point exactly. You don't *want* to learn math or science. You're deliberately trying to fail."

I almost jumped out of my chair. "What?"

"I'm not saying I'm the most perceptive person in the world, honey. But I do know that you're proud. Ordinarily, if

49

you were having serious trouble understanding a subject, you'd want to straighten it out, just to know that you could do it. But for some reason, you're just tuning this out. You're off in some—"

Before she could finish, the phone rang. I made a dash for it. Peter, who had an infallible sense of timing, had promised to call before dinner.

"Hi, there," he said cheerfully.

"Hi, Peter," I giggled back into the phone.

My mother shifted uneasily.

"Um, can you hold on for just a second?" I muffled the receiver. "Should I ask him to call back?"

She had already gotten up. "No," she said, glancing from her painting over my desk back to me. "But . . ." She sighed again. "We'll talk at dinner."

It was my turn to sigh when she left the room. She had nearly burst my bubble. Thank goodness Peter had come to the rescue.

"Is this a bad time?" he asked when I got back to him.

"Absolutely not. I was hoping you'd call. How's your cold?" What I didn't add was that this was the best possible time. It would give my mother a chance to calm down, and me a chance to put aside my own nagging guilt about school.

"Oh, it's much better, thanks. Listen, I have a proposition for you."

"Hmm. What kind of proposition?" I asked, twisting a single curl through my fingers.

"Well, it's sort of a date."

"Sort of?"

He cleared his throat. "I was just thinking . . . You've heard me talk about these two friends of mine, Andy Hanes and

Matt Forster?'' There was something unusual in his voice. ''But you haven't really met them yet, have you?''

''No,'' I answered. ''Not exactly.'' Meeting Peter's friends wasn't something I had looked forward to. They were the kind of people who still ignored me at school. And Peter had always acted so different when I saw him with them.

''I just thought maybe we could all go to the movies together,'' he continued. ''Like next Friday night?''

I grabbed a breath. ''You mean all four of us?''

''One, two, three, four,'' he counted.

''Why?'' It was the first thought that came to me. Why on earth would Peter be wanting to get me together with these friends of his, who had ignored me in the past and would probably continue to do so? And why ask them along on our date? Didn't he want to be alone with me anymore?

''I just thought . . .'' He started again. ''Well, *they're* my friends. And *you're* my friend. And I just want you all to get to know each other. But it's O.K. if you don't want to. I mean, I haven't mentioned it to them yet, so if you don't—''

''No, no. It sounds O.K. I'd love to meet them.'' *Someday,* I added silently. Maybe in five or ten years.

''Okay, then,'' he was saying. ''If you're sure you don't mind, I'll organize it. Anything you'd like to see?''

I barely heard. Andrew Hanes, Frazier High football star. Matthew Forster, genius. I had nothing in common with them. What would we talk about? They would hate me, and they'd tell Peter so. Maybe that was why he was arranging this torture session—to get their seal of approval for me, or—

''Julienne?''

''Oh. Yes.'' I pulled myself together. ''Which movie? It doesn't matter, Peter,'' I drawled, retreating to my most

Dorinda-like voice. It had been weeks since I'd done that. "Whatever you decide. It'll be . . . fun."

Even as Dorinda, I had to force the last word out. It wouldn't be fun. I had just gotten used to one teenage male at a time. How could I possibly handle three?

Chapter Eleven

I was a bundle of nerves while getting ready for Friday night. The more I thought about it, the more unfair—and crazy—this date seemed. I had accomplished so much in the last month: coming out of my fantasies, dating Peter, getting to know Blair better. Even entering the writing contest had been a big step. Why couldn't things just go on the way they were, with Peter and me, and maybe a touch of Blair and Stephen now and then?

By the time Peter rang the bell, I was a wreck. I could feel myself falling back into the old trap. The dream world seemed so much safer.

"Hello, Peter!" Mother greeted him. "Come on in."

"Thanks." He grinned, catching my eye.

Returning his glad-to-see-you smile, I almost forgot all about Matt and Andy. But when we got to the theater, I was very quickly reminded.

They were in line for *Fly by Day.* I had never seen such a mismatched pair of buddies. Big, blond Andy towered by one foot and a good fifty pounds or so over Matt, whose black-rimmed glasses and too-short slacks made him the picture of nerdiness. It was hard to believe they had been friends since fourth grade, until I saw Peter walk up to them. That was the answer. Lagging a pace or two behind, I could see right away that he was the bridge. Not as athletic and macho-looking as Andy, but less shy and more sure of himself than Matt, Peter provided the neutral middle ground.

"Julienne, I guess you and Matt know each other a little from math class," he said, bringing me up beside him. "And this is Andy Hanes, Mr. Touchdown himself."

For the first few seconds, neither of them responded to my smile and polite, "Glad to meet you." Their faces were blank. All they did was stare at me.

Then Andy extended his hand. I gave him mine. "Such a pleasure," he said, with a slight bow. Before I could blink, he had raised my fingers to his lips.

"Delighted," Matt chimed in with a deep bow of his own.

Were they making fun of me? I wasn't sure. All I knew was that it was kind of a relief just to play along and *not* be myself. So I slipped into my Queen Guinevere voice.

"The pleasure is mine," I told them.

After that, I couldn't go back. Vying for my favor like the Knights of the Round Table, Andy and Matt were making it far too easy for me to slip back into my old habit.

"After you," they said together, each holding open one of the theater's double doors for me.

Inside, Andy insisted I have a bag of caramel popcorn, and Matt was my escort down the aisle to our seats. As I settled in beside Peter, they both helped me off with my coat.

"Well. Where did you move here from, Julienne?" Andy asked as we waited for the movie to begin.

"Portland. We just came out last year."

Matt took his glasses off to clean them. "Do you like it?"

"Oh, it's great. So quiet—I love it," I lied. "In the city we were always so busy. Rushing through the traffic, shopping in big crowds, ugh!"

(I hadn't until this month stopped complaining to my mother about the boredom of suburban life.)

"Yes, I like the country best myself," Andy agreed, nodding thoughtfully. "Gives you room to grow."

Peter had barely said a word since we entered the theater. Stealing glances at him during the movie, I always found his features stony and cold. What was wrong? Not once after the lights went out did he put his arm around me or give me the soft little kisses on my temple, cheek, and earlobe that he normally did in movies. Was he mad at me? But why? Wasn't I getting along perfectly with his friends? Isn't that what he wanted?

I was still wondering what was going on as we left the theater. Then Matt suggested we stop by Luigi's for a pizza.

Peter looked pointedly at his watch. "It's ten-fifteen. I can't stay late. Tomorrow's my shift on the phones."

"No problem," Andy assured him. "We won't keep you out past your bedtime."

As we walked down to the restaurant, I put my hands in my coat pockets to keep them warm (since Peter wasn't holding either one of them), and only half-listened to Matt's analysis of the deep philosophical symbolism of the movie. Peter didn't say anything. Maybe he just felt uncomfortable with me around his friends. Why *had* he insisted on getting us together?

Matt and Andy didn't seem to notice his quietness. At

55

Luigi's they were still aking me about Portland, and where in the city I had lived.

"The last place we lived was near the river. It was nice." What I didn't mention was the leaky plumbing and the furnace that kept breaking down.

"Do you happen to know where Washington Street is?" Andy asked.

I searched my memory. Would I have to admit that although I had lived in the city most of my life I couldn't even find our old house when we had gone back a few months ago?

Matt saved me. "Don't tell me you're still trying to get that advanced Conquest manual, Andy."

"You guessed it. And don't roll your eyes at me. It could really shape up our game, if you, Mr. High and Mighty Game Master, would give it a chance."

"Look, Andy," Matt answered. "I've already seen that piece of—" Suddenly he stopped, and glanced at me. "Oh, well. No need to argue over it now. We can discuss this later."

"You guys are too much—" Peter began.

But Andy cut him off. "Matt's right. Let's talk about it later. We must be boring Julienne."

"Oh, no, I'm really interested in Conquest," I said. "Peter told me a little about it, but I'm not sure I understand how it works. Is it based totally on your imagination?"

"Absolutely," Matt confirmed. "It's a fantasy world."

Andy agreed.

Suddenly, for the first time that night, Peter perked up.

"Hey, I have a great idea," he said. "There's no reason why you can't come and find out for yourself next Saturday. Isn't that right, Game Master Forster?"

It fell like a bolt of lightning on the tiny table. The air crackled. What was going on with these guys? Why had Peter invited me to play Conquest with his friends when he'd obviously had such a lousy time tonight? And why were his friends suddenly acting so strange when they'd been so friendly all night?

All I heard was Andy mumble, then Matt clear his throat. He answered in a low voice.

"Sure. I guess so."

Chapter Twelve

I suppose something should have tipped me off about what lay ahead. Whenever I saw Peter that next week, and his friends happened to be around, he acted uncomfortable, while they continued to act like perfect gentlemen. I wanted to ask Peter what was going on, but I couldn't. Even though we were getting very close, there were some things I still couldn't talk about with him. His friends, for instance.

On Saturday, Peter and I spent the afternoon at my house sharing slice after slice of cranberry bread. Raindrops splattered against the big bay window in the breakfast nook. I had pushed away my worries about his strange behavior, because he always went back to normal when we were alone together.

Instead, I was thinking about the contest. It had been twenty-one days and two hours since I had mailed my entry. The station was scheduled to announce the winners the following week. Wasn't it about time I let Peter know about the contest? That way, he'd understand my depression when I lost. He had to be prepared.

So I squeezed his hand and smiled. "There's something I'd like to show you."

He grinned suspiciously. "Oh, yeah?"

"Yeah. You have to come upstairs."

"Uh-oh," he said, still grinning. "But my reputation—"

I pulled him up out of his chair. "I've got something for you to *read*, silly. Come on."

We trudged up the stairs and he plopped into my armchair, while I found the slim yellow folder in my filing cabinet.

"Shouldn't we leave the door open?" he asked, only half-joking.

I rolled my eyes and banged it shut. "You *know* my mother's not like that, Peter. Besides, this is a secret."

"What is?"

I swallowed. Despite all the certainty I'd felt a few moments ago, I was now uneasy about having someone I knew read over my work. I took a deep breath and paused to get up my courage—the way you do on the edge of a high-dive board—before I gave him the folder.

"This. It's my entry in the KWEB radio amateur playwright contest, for their Theater Hour. I—I just wanted you to have a look at it."

"Oh, yeah!" He cried enthusiastically as he opened the folder. "Hey, I heard about this. My sisters listen to that show all the time. You actually entered the contest?"

He had already started to flip through it.

"Wow! Twenty-five pages. This must've been a lot of work!"

"You don't have to read it now, if . . ."

His eyes flew up to mine. "No, I'd like to. We have a little time to kill before dinner at my house, anyway."

It took him forever to read it. While he did, I sat curled up in my windowseat, struggling not to watch him. I didn't really want to see the grimaces and smirks I feared he would be making. Instead, I tried to read a chapter of my chemistry book and ended up gazing out into the darkened street.

Finally, I heard him sigh, and looked over to see him put the last page in place. He kept staring down at the folder. I couldn't restrain myself.

"Well? What do you think?"

He looked up at me. Actually, I couldn't tell if it was at me or at the rain outside. "It's . . . heavy."

My stomach flopped over. *Heavy?* "You mean, it's . . ."

He focused back on the folder and drummed his fingers on the arm of the chair. I thought I would go crazy. Why couldn't he say something?

"You don't have to be polite, Peter. I can take it."

"Oh, no," he said gently, and got up. The few seconds it took for him to cross the room and settle in beside me passed like hours. Holding both my hands, he continued.

"Julienne, it's just that . . . you write so well. I had no idea. I'm really . . . impressed."

There was something he wasn't telling me. I could see it in his eyes. Something like, "What a shame you sent in this crock of hogwash," or, "Don't you have better things to do?" He didn't have the heart to tell me how awful it was.

Suddenly, all my old insecurities came back. Here he was again, brooding about something that he couldn't or wouldn't tell me about. Only this time his friends weren't around. This time it was strictly between Peter and me. And I didn't dare ask what he was thinking.

When he lifted my chin with one gentle finger, and began with just the lightest, most feathery touches of his lips on mine, I should have known all the answers.

Chapter Thirteen

"We're beginning a whole new game tonight, O.K.? So we're all equal."

Matt sat at the head of the big oak table in the Garroways' den, dealing out cards and presiding over Conquest like a Supreme Court judge.

I had to smile. He and Peter and Andy were acting like kids, busily preparing for their favorite game. They went on explaining the rules to me, all the while giving me little figures that represented armies and weapons and who knew what else.

With the fire that Peter and I had built crackling in the hearth, I was beginning to feel almost relaxed again, forgetting all the silly fears I had had about Peter's feelings toward me. All that had been erased. Dinner with his family had been fun, and then afterwards, alone in the den, a big pillow fight on the couch had let out all my tension and given me a long, delicious laugh. Even Andy and Matt coming in to discover me sitting on top of Peter, tickling him to distraction, hadn't upset me.

"Now," Matt dictated, "since the object of the game is, of course, conquest, you want to occupy as many of these sectors as possible. Korlon One, the world that this map represents, is rich with valuable resources."

"The cards Matt dealt you," Peter added, "start you out in possession of sectors in three different regions."

"Yeah," Andy broke in. "Your armies and weapons are really spread out, so you should pick a sector that you can move toward and join forces . . ."

Although it was just mumbo-jumbo at first, I did my best to understand. Peter and his friends were trying so hard to get me involved that I didn't want to disappoint them. I began to fall into the fantasy of Korlon One.

"Okay now," Matt counseled on my third turn, "a good thing to do would be for you to go into Pete's Mafren sector."

"Be a sport, Pete," Andy urged. "All she's got to attack with is that puny little one-gun Range Roamer, anyway."

That was when I started feeling uneasy. I didn't think that my Range Roamer was so puny. And I had a plan for getting more weapons.

"Now," Matt said, after I had taken over Mafren, "Bartad sector."

Andy shook his head. "No way! Go soak your head, Forster."

They bickered on as if I didn't exist. It made no difference that *my* armies and weapons and strategy were at stake, or that I knew perfectly well by now how to use them. I couldn't help feeling annoyed. I even tried hard not to. My mother would feel annoyed. She would demand to make her own decisions. She would complain about their patronizing and dominating and interfering. And no matter what, I didn't want to sound like my mother.

I concentrated on the game.

Over the next few turns, I began to think the problem was that the boys thought I wasn't really interested. Peter looked distracted, doodling little pictures of frogs on his pad, and Andy and Matt became too involved in their war on each other to give me more than passing comments. That situation left me free to add gun after gun to the power of my weapons. I moved into small, insignificant little sectors that no one cared about. That no one *seemed* to care about.

After about an hour, I was prepared for my big move. I had decided to show them all that I really was interested in Conquest. I wanted Peter, especially, to feel proud of me.

"Your turn," Andy informed me, yawning.

I surveyed my positions. My strategy seemed right—perfect.

I made my challenge. "Quetar Sector attacks Tantin Region," I announced.

A silence fell over the table. Then it all came out in a flood.

"Tantin Region! You're crazy! That's mine," Andy thundered.

"You cannot even attempt to take an entire region," Matt warned, "unless you've got at least two sixth-power-level weapons and—"

Before he could go on, I showed him. I didn't have two sixth-power-level weapons. I had four.

Beaming proudly, I expected equally proud smiles in return. After all, I was their protégé. But when I looked up, I saw Mount St. Helens, in the form of Andy Hanes, ready to blow. I saw Matt Forster, a buzzing hornet. And I saw Peter, *my* Peter, laughing.

He was *laughing* at me! This was all a joke to him.

He was laughing so hard he could barely talk. "Pretty impressive, huh, guys? Not bad for a first-timer."

Andy ripped the point tally out of my hand. "It's impossible!" Matt agreed. Why didn't they believe me?

"But I've kept track—" I began.

"So have I!" Matt flung back. He was double-checking my tally, frowning and chewing his lower lip.

I couldn't understand. I had only tried to please them, to show them how well I had learned. Then I remembered. That feeling I'd had just before my attack—what had it been? Courage? Power? The kind of feeling my mother said she sometimes had in board meetings and sales presentations and . . .

I didn't want that.

I took a deep breath. "It doesn't matter. I don't have to attack there."

Andy interrupted me. "What do you mean, you don't have to? If you've got the guns, you have to, by the rules."

Then Peter spoke up. "Hey, come on, folks. It's just a game."

"Yeah. Just a game," Andy snarled. "Unless people start cheating."

It was a thousand volts, at least—an electric shock in my brain. And then my head swam. I felt dizzy, and the three of them sitting at the table made a hazy blur.

"Yeah, cheating," Andy repeated, with Matt nodding his head.

I might have been able to stay calm if it hadn't been for the fact that Peter was just sitting there, letting them accuse me. I had to do something.

"I don't cheat!" I screamed at them.

For a second, it seemed that no one heard or cared.

Then Matt asked, "Then how could you possibly do so well so soon?"

"I just played." My voice was low and shaky. "By your rules."

The expression that appeared on Matt's face was more of a grimace than a smile. Andy was peering at me suspiciously out of the corner of his eye. How could they do this to me? Just the day before, they had been perfect gentlemen!

Peter reached out and circled my forearm with his fingers. "Hey," he said, smiling at me and speaking in a soft, infuriating voice, "why don't we just calm down."

Calm down. The words cut through me. He was telling *me* to calm down and hardly saying a word to his friends. Didn't he see what they were doing?

A moment before, I had been far too angry to cry. I had wanted to rip their stupid game board in two, but the last thing I had wanted was to give them the satisfaction of tears.

Now, I couldn't help it. Not trusting my voice with another word, I grabbed up my jacket and ran.

Chapter Fourteen

Running out of Peter's house, I had only one purpose: to get away from him and his so-called friends. Suddenly, I thought I understood things that had made no sense before. I hurried down the street, telling myself that Andy and Matt had never really liked me at all. They had just been pretending, for Peter's sake, and now their real feelings about me had finally come out.

Maybe that was why Peter had been so uncomfortable around them. He had known how they really felt all along. Or, on the other hand, maybe Peter had been putting me through some kind of test with his friends. And I had failed. But why? Wasn't what he and I had together enough? Why did he have to drag his friends into it?

And why hadn't he stood up for me? The question whirled around in my brain. I didn't know what to think or feel anymore. I should have stayed on Channel DREAM, I thought, where things made sense. My confusion burst out in a fresh flood of tears.

It wasn't until I turned the corner to my street, running, that I heard Peter on the sidewalk behind me.

"Julienne, wait!"

I hadn't expected him. Wasn't he glad to get rid of me? Wasn't that what he had been trying to do?

I stopped and turned to face him, not realizing that he was right at my heels. He took my shoulders in his hands and held me in front of him. I didn't even try to pull away. We just stood there in the cold, staring at each other.

"Julienne," he finally said. "Those two were just acting up. You shouldn't let them get to you." He sounded like a grade school teacher settling a disagreement on the playground.

"*Get* to me?" I repeated, starting to tremble. "Peter, they —they—I don't cheat!" I had stifled my tears, but could feel them welling up again.

"Heck, I know that, Julienne. Of course you don't. But that's not the point. They just—"

"They raked me over the coals!" I burst out.

Squeezing my shoulders, Peter tried to hold me closer, but I wouldn't let him.

"Listen. You don't know them. Andy and Matt are like that. They're not worth crying over."

But it's not just them, I wanted to say. *I'm crying because I don't know you.*

"Why don't we go back and get them to apologize, and just forget the whole thing?" he said with a hopeful look.

"Go back!" I managed to sputter.

"Well, sure. They'll come to their senses."

For a few seconds, I didn't know what to say. How could he be so casual about this? Did he really expect me to simply walk back to those creeps and be all smiles again?

Searching his face, I saw the intensity in his eyes and the

concern that was making the little dimple in his chin deeper than ever. I just couldn't believe that he really wanted to hurt me. And I was tired of going around in circles trying to figure out what was going on inside his head. It was time to give him the benefit of the doubt and to bring everything into the open, once and for all.

"I won't go back there tonight, Peter," I said as calmly as I could.

He sighed, puffing his cheeks out and letting his breath out slowly. "Yeah, O.K. I can understand that. But really, you've got to know that the way they acted tonight was nothing personal."

I shook my head. "Then you don't understand yet, do you? Andy and Matt have never liked me. They were just acting nice for—for your sake. Can't you see that they wanted to drive me out tonight?" I looked away. "They want someone better for you."

"Someone better? Julienne, is that what you really think?"

"Yes," I said firmly. "When you and I were first getting to know each other"—my heart took a little leap as I said the words—"you'd ignore me whenever they were around, remember? Don't think I didn't notice. It was because of them, wasn't it?"

He grimaced and turned away sheepishly. "Well, in a way, but . . ."

That confession made me cringe, but I went on. It was time to face facts. "You wanted to get their approval. That's why you've been forcing us all together, and—"

"No! Hold on a minute," he interrupted. "I don't need their approval for anything."

"Then why did you insist on getting us all together, when it's clear that they can't stand me?"

"You're wrong about that, Julienne. Matt and Andy don't hate you. I know that for a fact. They like you fine."

"Well, then, what happened tonight?" I rushed on. "Why did they . . . attack me?"

"First things first. I wasn't out to get anyone's approval by bringing you all together. But, well . . ." He looked down. "You're right about one thing. At first I was worried about them not getting along with you. They thought . . . well, you didn't socialize much and I guess they thought you weren't very friendly. I was afraid they'd do or say something stupid, like they did tonight, and get you mad at me. But I knew that once they met you and spent time with you, they'd change their minds. And they did. They've admitted they were wrong about you."

"I don't know if I can believe that."

"But they did, really. The reason they blew up tonight is because . . ."

I waited while he struggled for words.

"It has to do with the way you played Conquest."

"The way I . . . But I was trying so hard to do well, to please them . . ."

He shrugged. "You did do well. It was pretty darned impressive. And that was the problem."

His face flushed dark red. I'd never seen him look so pained.

"I hate to say it, Julienne. But my friends, those guys I grew up with, are real male chauvinist pigs. When it comes down to it, they . . . See, they didn't like it when you did so well."

I remembered that feeling of triumph I'd had during the game—and the worry that had come with it.

"They've still got this idea that girls really shouldn't be as competitive and everything as guys, and when you started beating them at their own game, they went nuts."

Suddenly, he broke into a sly grin.

I was horrified.

"Do you think that's funny?" I demanded.

"No—oh, listen, I'm sorry. What I'm happy about is how good you got them. You really stuck it to them tonight with that maneuver. They need to be shaken up like that more often."

"But Peter, I wasn't trying to shake anyone up. I just . . . I thought . . ." Pulling myself together, I began again. "I thought I was doing what they wanted, and what *you* wanted. You always seemed so upset around them, and then tonight—"

"O.K.," he said, sighing again. "I'll confess that I knew something like this would happen tonight during that game. I guess I sort of planned it. See, Julienne, I knew Andy and Matt weren't very realistic when it came to girls. They treat them like well, like delicate flowers most of the time. And I knew you weren't really like that, but when those guys were around you acted like you really enjoyed the way they were treating you. So I thought I'd give you all a chance to *really* get to know each other a little bit," he said, with a grin.

He threw his shoulders back proudly, as if he had just done me a tremendous favor. Watching his satisfied expression, I suddenly had no desire to cry. Another feeling was coming over me—one just as unpleasant. Things were beginning to fall into place.

"Do you mean you actually *planned* for Andy and Matt to turn on me, Peter?"

"No, of course not. I didn't know they'd act *that* stupid. But I knew that Conquest would make them act normal around you for a change. It wasn't natural for them to be so polite all the time. I knew that a good game of Conquest would make them stop holding you up on a pedestal, and that it would let you come down off it."

I had to search for my voice. "What . . . pedestal?"

"Well . . . take your story, for instance." He was right in front of me, but somehow I felt he was a mile away. "What bothered me about it is that you've got the heroine, Rebecca,

70

who is perfectly intelligent and capable. But the hero, Reed, is always having to come along and rescue her from all kinds of things." He mumbled out some vague compliment about my writing and then came up with the clincher. "But life doesn't happen that way, Julienne."

A wave of prickly heat washed over me. I could feel my cheeks blushing, and my heart begin to pound. It was as if Peter had just lifted the lid to my soul and was poking it with a stick.

"I mean, sometimes I get the idea that you really believe all that stuff about guys being knights in shining armor looking for damsels in distress."

A thousand little hairs along my spine stood on end. He *knew* about my dream world. At first I felt squirmy and embarrassed, as if I had been caught with the cookie jar. But as he went on, I felt humiliated—and angry.

"You really did like the way Andy and Matt treated you before today, right? You couldn't see that all that polite stuff was part of the problem."

I couldn't hold back a second longer. "At least they were nice to me then!" I blurted out.

"Maybe it seemed that way," he insisted. "But remember, they were only nice while you acted like a little fairy-tale princess."

Finally I exploded. "So you set this all up! You deliberately set up that game just to teach me a lesson?"

He came toward me. "Julienne, I didn't mean for you to get hurt."

"Why didn't you just come out and *tell* me how you felt?"

"Would you have listened?" he asked, raising an eyebrow. "You seemed so taken in by Andy and Matt that I didn't think warning you would do any good."

He had all his excuses ready and waiting.

"I see," I nodded, trying to control my voice. "You just

71

decided to conduct a harmless little experiment, with me as the guinea pig. A shy, lonely, mixed-up girl—the perfect subject—used to teach your friends a thing or two, as well!''

"It wasn't like that, Julienne. You don't understand. I just wanted to help you!"

To help me. Not to love me, or to enjoy being with me. But to help me.

"I don't need that kind of help," I tossed out, fighting back tears. "What I need is—is—" The tears choked me off.

"Julienne, please. Listen."

"Listen to what? More of your preaching?" I blubbered. "You have no right to try to change me, Peter!"

"But that's not what I was trying to do, Julienne! I was—"

He stopped and shook his head.

I was suddenly so cold and tired and miserable that I couldn't stand another second of this. All I wanted was to curl up by myself and forget tonight had ever happened.

"Oh, just leave me alone!" I screamed, and ran away from him into my house.

Chapter Fifteen

In *Dark Flower of Love* or *Raging Tide of Passion*, Peter would have come running after me, swept me into his arms, and kissed me so perfectly that we both would have immediately forgotten all our differences.

That wasn't Real Life.

In real life, I cried myself to sleep and spent most of Sunday alone in my room, trying to hate him. At school on Monday, I skipped lunch and avoided everywhere I thought he might be. By that afternoon, I was curled up in my windowseat, still trying to sort my feelings.

Peter had tricked me, hadn't he? Knowing full well what could happen, he had set me up to be picked on by his friends. He was even proud of it, seeing himself as a missionary spreading the truth to all his misguided friends.

I did a hundred instant replays of our fight, trying to

recapture all the anger I had felt. But it just wasn't there.

No matter how I tried to turn my heart against Peter, it wouldn't go. What it kept remembering were all the wonderful times we had spent together. The tender way he looked at me, his rumbling laugh, the soft, sweet touch of his lips on mine . . .

How could I throw away a whole month of that just because of one bad day?

Deep down, I knew he hadn't meant to hurt me. I couldn't believe that he didn't feel something for me. Instead of running away from him, I should have stayed and listened to all he had to say.

I shut my eyes, remembering that my own feelings of shame and humiliation were what had made me run. I had felt low and worthless and stupid. I was sure that Peter saw me as a pitiful charity case, and not as someone he could respect and admire . . . and love.

That's what I would have been mad about, if it hadn't been for the fact that his plan had worked. I was ashamed of the way I had let Andy and Matt bully me into backing out of my challenge during the Conquest game. I began to realize that there was still a lot I had to learn about boys—and about life.

Wasn't that what my mother was always saying? That I had to be prepared?

With a heavy sigh, I hugged my knees and rested my chin on them. I had come a long way in four weeks. Real life was even more complicated than I had feared, but here I was, coping with it and at least trying to face it head-on. And oddly enough, I felt more calm than I had in months.

So, I asked myself, *what happens next?* Now that I had my own feelings ironed out (somewhat), wasn't it time to get on the phone and find out what Peter's were? Wasn't that what a mature, modern, real-life girl would do?

I knew it was what I should do. But I still had my doubts. I couldn't get the image of Peter as a social worker out of my mind. Would I be able to handle the pain that would come if it turned out that he did see me as a charity case? Or would I learn that he really cared about me as *me*?

I didn't have a chance to decide, because the doorbell rang. For a moment, I just sat there, hypnotized. It rang again. And then, suddenly, I was sure.

It was Peter.

I must have rocketed down the stairs. It was all ready, on the tip of my tongue: *Peter, I'm sorry. I shouldn't have run away from you. Let's talk over our problems. You were right about so many things.*

But the person on the doorstep couldn't have cared less who I was, as long as my last name matched the one on the envelope he was delivering.

"Registered letter, miss. Sign right here, please."

It wasn't until I had scrawled out my signature, mumbled, "Thanks," and shut the door that I saw the logo in the upper lefthand corner of the cream-colored envelope.

KWEB-FM PUBLIC RADIO: THE LISTENER'S CHOICE

I had to support myself against the wall. Poring over the envelope, I made absolutely sure that it was addressed to me, and not to my mother or to any of the neighbors. I couldn't believe it had really come to the right person. Next, I was overcome by a fit of most un-Lady Eleanor-like hysteria, during which I tore open the flap and whipped out the letter.

My eyes flew over it.

We are delighted to inform you ... your radio drama ... HOPE FOR LOVE ... selected ... Theater Hour contest ... third prize ...

I was still trembling when my mother bustled in a minute or two later.

75

"Hi, pumpkin. I just saw the mail truck drive off. Anything for me?"

I looked up at her, still half in shock. The remaining half of my brain was racing to figure out whether or not to tell her.

Wouldn't she be proud and pleased? *My daughter, the writer,* she could say. Or she could say, *My daughter, who must go out and try to make a living with such unmarketable skills.*

"Honey, what's wrong? Is it something..." Her voice trailed off anxiously. She looked so pale and stricken that I couldn't keep it from her any longer. She was going to have to know, sooner or later.

I held the letter out to her.

With her head bowed and her giant reading glasses eclipsing her eyes, I couldn't see what she was thinking. I watched her in silence, dying to let loose with a yodel of joy. Instead, I knew I had to prepare for the worst.

For an eternity, I waited. Finally she began to shake her head. My heart stopped.

"Julienne, this is... why, this is marvelous."

Marvelous?

The next thing I knew she was snatching her glasses off and turning all the sparkle in her blue eyes on me.

"Absolutely wonderful! I'm so proud of you, honey! So this is what you were burning the midnight oil for, is it?"

I nodded vaguely.

"Oh, goodness gracious!" She put her glasses back on to reread the letter. "You're going to tell me all about this over dinner at the Sandpiper tonight. This deserves a real celebration!"

I wanted to let all my doubts go, but couldn't.

76

"You mean you're not . . . upset?" I stammered.

Her eyebrows knitted together. "Upset?"

"Well, about my entering the contest?"

"Julienne, how could I possibly be upset?" she laughed. "I'm so *proud* of you!"

Scooping me into her arms, she gave me a tight, jubilant squeeze. Then she held me away from her.

"Honey, did you really think I wouldn't share your joy over this?"

"Well, I . . . I thought you didn't want me to write."

"Didn't want you to—" She stopped and shook her head. "Oh, honey. I never meant to give you that idea."

In her eyes I saw all the real pride and love she felt for me.

"Why, I couldn't be happier if you had singlehandedly solved the world's hardest trigonometry problem," she laughed. "This is a real achievement. And you're going to go on achieving in your writing. I know you are."

"But you've always said it wasn't . . . marketable. And that I shouldn't waste my time—"

"Julienne, I never meant to imply that writing was a waste of your time."

I saw her crooked, sheepish grin. "But it looks like I gave you that impression, doesn't it?"

She took my hand in hers.

"Let's sit down for a minute."

Side by side on the bottom step, I felt more in tune with her than I had in years.

"I treasure this talent of yours, Julienne. And so should you. It seems I went overboard a little in trying to steer you toward technical skills. I just wanted to make sure you don't have to *depend* on an artistic talent to make your way through life. You need to have all the information and skills you can get. Do you agree?"

I nodded. "I think so. But I'm still not crazy about Mr. Hoff's trigonometry."

Mother smiled and hugged me. "As long as you don't shut it out—as long as you give it your best, you're on your way. But don't ever think, honey, that I won't approve of your artistic efforts as well. Just because I couldn't make a career out of painting doesn't mean you won't find one with your writing talent."

"You really think that's true?" I asked, feeling a grateful tear or two sting my eyes.

"Absolutely," she reassured me.

"And you really think I should keep trying?"

She held up the KWEB letter. "What do you think this means? Now scoot and get ready. We're heading for the fanciest eatery this side of Portland."

Gazing at the letter on my way upstairs, I was flooded with joy. I had never dreamed I would actually win anything in the contest. I just wanted to make the effort. Coming down out of the clouds had brought me far. Now things were working out. My mother and I were finally airing our feelings, and I was even beginning to understand myself better. But one big chunk of the puzzle was still out of place.

A sharp pain cut through me as I thought of Peter. I wanted more than anything to call and share the news with him. But it would seem so hypocritical to yell and scream at him one minute, then expect him to be wild with joy for me the next. And I still had some thinking to do about how I was going to approach him.

For tonight, I would try to forget about all that. I would go out and enjoy myself, and put off facing Peter for just one more day. Because it wasn't going to be easy.

I wanted to believe that I could just walk back into his life (from which I had so recently stormed out) and say: *Peter, a miracle has occurred! I've won third place in the contest.*

Let's forget all the horrid things we said to each other, and celebrate!

As much as I wanted to believe it could be so simple, I knew that was just another fairy tale. And I had promised, deep in my heart, that I would never get lost in one again.

Chapter Sixteen

"Julienne! Heels down! All the way! Concentrate!"

I couldn't concentrate. Not on Mirage, who I was riding, or on Gregory, who only a month ago could have hypnotized me. All I could think about was the fact that today, right after my lesson, I was going to set things straight with Peter.

"Balance, Julienne, balance!"

Even after the heart-to-heart talk with my mother and our dinner out last night, I hadn't been able to sleep. I had tossed and turned, trying to decide what to say to him.

"Your hands are too flat!" Gregory roared. "Bring them out."

Of course, I could have told myself that Peter was the one who should come to me. If Andy and Matt could just walk right up to me (as they had today after lunch) and mumble apologies, then why couldn't he? After all, he was every bit as responsible for our feud as they were. But I wanted to take the step myself, to prove to us both that I was facing life realistically.

"Now, you're going to jump the first cavaletti. And you're going to think, concentrate on every move."

Taking Mirage around to the lowest obstacle, I caught a glimpse of tall, dark Gregory's glacial blue eyes and remembered how quickly I had forgotten them in favor of Peter's laughing, lake-colored ones. His lean lankiness, his honey blond hair, his . . .

As Mirage and I sailed over the jump, I saw those eyes and that hair and those long legs, plain as day, beside the cabin.

"Hands forward! Let her have her head!"

Gregory's command made my eyes move. And when I turned them back, Peter was gone. *Stop dreaming*, I scolded myself.

Precisely at four forty-five, the end of our hour, Gregory stalked out of the ring. I dismounted and led Mirage back to Laura.

My plan was to call Peter as soon as I got home and ask to meet with him after dinner. *We need to talk this out*, I would say sensibly. *I won't run away again*. One way or another, I would learn how he felt.

"You going out the main gate, Julienne?" Laura asked.

"Yes." It struck me as an odd question. I always went out the main gate.

"Oh. O.K.," she smiled. "Have a good week!"

Maybe that should have been a hint. Looking back, I realize that there were clues all around me: the crystalline winter blue that had sliced the clouds to let in a spray of late sunshine; the warmth of it on my back, reminding me that my silly fairy-tale writing had actually won a contest; and the lone daisy, lying cut and abandoned, right in the middle of the gravel path.

Maybe I should have suspected something, but I was still too absorbed in thinking out my upcoming talk with Peter. Nothing tipped me off until I heard the loud whinny behind me. Glancing back, I expected to see Laura with one of the boarder horses. But it wasn't a boarder. And it wasn't Laura. To this day, I wonder how I kept from collapsing in shock. Because plodding up behind me was an old, gray-dappled horse—my first training mount, led by a tall, smiling boy— my first love.

"My dearest Lady Julienne," Peter said with a straight face, as he and the horse stopped in front of me. "Whose lovely name I have heardeth announced on the radio." He cracked a smile at that part, but went on. "My dearest, brilliant contest winner." He dropped to one knee. One hand was on his heart holding a bouquet of daisies, and the other held Ranger's reins. His eyes were turned up to mine.

"In humble apology for the unpardonable antics of my boorish, oafish associates, as well as for my own demented ravings, I am most humbly devoted to your—"

He was interrupted by Ranger, who lowered his big head and casually nipped at the flowers.

"Why, you—!" Peter began, trying to whip them out of the horse's reach. But it was too late. Shrugging, he gave Ranger the stems. Then, he rolled his eyes and continued.

"I am most humbly devoted to your service, m'lady. At your command, at your whim, and at your beck and call, I am yours." He swept my hand up to his lips.

It was far too good to be true. Was Peter really coming back to me? His kiss on my palm tickled so deliciously that I had to laugh out loud, which made him lift his head and crack into that wonderful, chin-dimpled grin of his. Looking down on his beaming, upturned face and wind-tousled hair, and feeling his hand on mine, I began to believe it was happening. He *was* coming back to me.

There was only one thing to do. I dropped down to my knees, placed my free hand over my heart, and composed myself.

"Sir Peter, oh, noble lord. Both honored and dismayed am I by your plea. 'Twas I—oh!'' I dropped my eyes. " 'Twas I, m'lord, who taxed you, who vexed and provoked you. Nay, you must never again speak of your guilt.''

"Nay! I shall, fair Julienne. For I—'' His voice collapsed in a chuckle. "For cripes sake, Julienne, I've got to talk normal for a minute.''

Neither of us moved.

"You're too important to me,'' he said, twining his fingers with mine, "to let you go so easily. You told me to leave you alone, so, like a fool, I did. But last night, when I heard you'd won the contest, I couldn't stay away anymore. I acted like a jerk, Julienne. Andy and Matt acted like jerks. And you were right. I had no right to try to change you three in the first place.''

Pulling myself together, I tried to remember all the things I had planned to say to him. "But I could use some changing,'' was all that came out.

Peter shook his head. "I want you the way you are, Julienne. I always have. Ever since you first came to Frazier last year, I've been thinking about you.''

"You have?''

"Yes, ma'am,'' he said.

My heart was wild. He was so close—his own heart beating just inches from mine, and his breath making little clouds to mix with mine—that I could barely think.

"I'm really sorry about putting you through the ringer with Andy and Matt. Honest, I never thought they'd get that rowdy. I just . . ." He shrugged hopelessly. "Somehow I got the idea if I could make those two jerks grow up a little . . . Oh, I don't know anymore what I thought."

I had to smile. "They did go overboard," I said. "But I want you to know, Peter, that I . . . my own behavior wasn't very smart, either. I guess I really did let them intimidate me during that game. If I had just laughed them off—"

"They would have backed down like the lily-livered chickens they really are."

I laughed with him. "Really?"

"I guarantee."

He looked so sorry that I wanted to snuggle into his arms. But first I had to get all my doubts out of the way.

"Peter, you're not . . . you're not just interested in me as, well, someone to . . ." I looked away, trying to force the words out. "Someone you can help. I mean, you don't think I'm a . . ."

His puzzled frown suddenly turned into a grin.

"A fruitcake? Sure I do. And I love fruitcakes. Honest." His voice softened as he kissed the tip of my nose.

Then he took both of my hands in his and held them up between us. We drew together and our lips met halfway, it seemed, over our clasped hands, and between all we had yet to say to each other. It was a warm, long kiss, fevered by our sense of discovery. It was a truce.

"Game over?" he whispered.

I nodded lazily, still a little dizzy. "Absolutely. Ending in a tie. Joint, mutual conquest."

His eyes were lit up, he drew nearer, and I was sure he was going to kiss me again. But Ranger shook his head and snorted impatiently.

"Oh, yeah," Peter told him. "I almost forgot."

He jumped to his feet.

"Shall we go?" He gestured toward the horse.

"On Ranger? Where?"

"Off into the sunset, of course," he announced, coaxing me to my feet.

True to his word, the sky's blue had faded to golds and reds.

"A short ride, m'lady, for your pleasure."

"But only with you, m'lord," I insisted.

"Me?"

He looked stricken as I swung into the saddle and held out my hand.

"Oh, no," he protested. "I don't know how to—"

"I'll take the reins," I assured him.

"Well, in that case . . ." He climbed up behind me.

Guiding Ranger onto the path, I felt the warmth of Peter's breath in my ear.

"Jolly good sport, m'lady, with you at the helm."

It was no fairy tale. I could no longer believe, as I once had, that Peter and I would never disagree or misunderstand each other, or that all I needed was a good imagination and a valiant knight to protect me. Peter—and my mother—had been right about some things. I had to know how to stand up and face reality.

On the other hand, I couldn't quite believe that what I was feeling now was just a regular part of humdrum, everyday Real Life. It was special, and every bit as magical as anything I had ever read about.

That was the unexpected part, I realized as I settled back into Peter's arms. Because if I had stayed in that dream world, safe and isolated, I never would have found out about all the exciting, romantic, and wonderful things that could really happen.

Smiling, I was lulled by Ranger's gentle, rocking walk and the steady beat of Peter's heart against my back. Somehow, I decided with a sigh, this kind of real life had always been only a dream away.

EVERY LOVE STORY HAS TWO SIDES...

PETER'S STORY . . .

So why . . . was I thinking about asking out Julienne Kelsey? She was nothing at all like the girls I dated before. Matt and Andy both thought Julienne was strange. But she seemed mysterious to me.

Peter usually goes for girls who are independent and down-to-earth, but Julienne is the dreamy type who seems to expect boys to act like the heroes in the romantic books she's always reading. There's something about her that Peter can't resist, though, no matter how much his friends razz him about dating her. If only he could find a way to show his buddies what a terrific girl Julienne really is. And if only he could find a way to make Julienne realize that she's as smart and capable as any boy. But when Peter *does* think of a game plan, to do both those things, he almost loses his best friends—*and his girlfriend*—in one night . . .

TWO BY TWO ROMANCES™ are designed to show you both sides of each special love story in this series. You get two complete books in one. Read what it's like for a boy to fall in love. Then turn the book over and find out what love means to the girl.

Peter's story begins on page one of this half of ONLY A DREAM AWAY. Does Julienne feel the same way? Flip the book over and read her story to find out.

You'll Want to Read All the Books in the
TWO BY TWO ROMANCE™ Series

October 1983 Publication
#1 CASSIE & CHRIS   (D30-801, $1.95, U.S.A.)
by Sara Casey   (D30-936, $2.25, Canada)

Cassie's parents won't let her date until she's fifteen. Chris is in big trouble—for something he didn't do—and his parents refuse to let him see his friends. But Cassie finds lots of time to see Chris in school, and before he knows it, Chris is caught up in Cassie's crazy plan to keep them together!

October 1983 Publication
#2 JED & JESSIE   (D30-802, $1.95, U.S.A.)
by Abby Connell   (D30-937, $2.25, Canada)

In the three years she'd been away, Jessie had changed a lot. How could she make people see she wasn't the tough little kid they remembered? How was Jed supposed to know that the tough little neighborhood girl he had ignored was going to turn into someone as special and beautiful as Jessica Kearns?

November 1983 Publication
#3 CHANGE OF HEART   (D30-803, $1.95, U.S.A.)
by Patricia Aks   (D30-970, $2.25, Canada)

Betsey, the first girl editor of the school newspaper, is having a hard time getting along with Eric, the sports photographer for the paper. Eric has always wanted to be an artist, but now he has to take orders from "Boss" Betsey. So why can't they stop thinking about each other?

December 1983 Publication
#4 ONLY A DREAM AWAY   (D30-804, $1.95, U.S.A.)
by Kathryn Makris   (D32-022, $2.25, Canada)

Julienne: "What does it matter if I'm not Miss Popularity? I can get by without football games and proms and boys—as long as I have my books." Peter: "Julienne was nothing at all like the girls I dated before. My friends think she's strange. But she seems mysterious to me." What happens when a dreamy girl and a down-to-earth guy get together?

January 1984 Publication
#5 ONE SPECIAL SUMMER   (D30-805, $1.95, U.S.A.)
by Janice Harrell   (D32-080, $2.25, Canada)

Take another look, Mac. Your best friend's kid sister is not such a kid anymore! This is your time, Polly, to show Mac that Pearce's little sister is a big girl now!

All kinds of possibilities raced through my mind. What kind of misunderstanding were we going to have next?

"—as someone you can help," she continued. "I mean, you don't think I'm a..." She looked away, as if she couldn't bear to finish.

As someone I could help? Finally I understood. Maybe she thought I was just stringing her along on some sort of ego trip, and didn't really care about her. It was such a nutty, impossible thing for her to come up with that I decided she deserved just a little bit of teasing.

"...a fruitcake?" I finished for her. "Sure I do. And I love fruitcakes. Honest." And I gave her a little kiss on the tip of her nose.

And then, finally, came the kiss that made me believe everything in the whole world was perfect and right-side-up again.

"Game over?" I asked as we parted.

"Absolutely," she whispered. "Ending in a tie. Joint, mutual conquest."

I was just getting ready to kiss her again, when I felt old Ranger tugging on the reins, reminding me about the rest of my plan.

"Oh, yeah. I almost forgot." Reluctantly, I pulled away from Julienne and stood up.

"Shall we go?" I pointed at the horse.

"On Ranger?" She looked horrified. "Where?"

It was corny, but just this once, I wanted to give her the kind of stuff she dreamed about. "Off into the sunset, of course! A short ride, m'lady, for your pleasure."

She looked at me with a wicked grin.

"But only with you, m'lord."

"Me? You mean you want me to actually ride that horse?"

She did. Already on Ranger's back, she reached toward me to help me up.

"Oh, no. I don't know how to—"

Somehow, she conned me into getting up on that old nag with her, which wasn't really such a bad place to be, considering the fact that I got to keep my arms around her the whole time. She snuggled back into my arms and sighed, leaving me free to hug her close and bury my face in the spicy apple smell of her hair.

"Jolly good sport, m'lady, with you at the helm."

I shut my eyes and breathed her in, relieved to have back her velvet brown eyes and her moodiness and her Mona Lisa smile. In spite of all the things I had said to her about being off in a dream world, I really admired the way her imagination could float her off into the wild stuff she wrote about. Julienne was talented, a little crazy sometimes, and definitely one of a kind.

And that, I think, is exactly why I loved her.

4

TWO BY TWO
ROMANCE™

Only
A Dream Away

Kathryn Makris

WARNER BOOKS

A Warner Communications Company

To Gavin, my love and inspiration, for believing.

Only
A Dream Away

PETER'S STORY

Chapter One

I should start with the fact that I have three older sisters. No brothers. So I got lots of attention when I was growing up. My friend Andy can't understand how sisters can be. His is just a couple of years older than he is, and his favorite story is about how she once tried to poke his eyes out with a fork. But Colleen, the youngest girl in my family, is six years older than I am, and she treated me like some kind of treasure when I was little. Suzanne and Lilly went bonkers over me, too. And the result is that I've always felt O.K. around girls. Always. In fact, I've always felt *great* around them.

Still, the one thing I don't think I'll ever understand is how, at age sixteen, I fell in love with Julienne Kelsey. The truth is that I'd fallen for lots of girls before. That was a habit of mine. But Julienne was almost totally different from every single one of the others.

My first love was Holly Marshall. I remember her clearly.

Short brown hair and dark eyes. A little pixie nose and dimples. She was almost six. I was five and a half. After I kissed her on the cheek and told her she was pretty, she wouldn't talk to me.

The next year she moved out of Webber Falls, so I guess it didn't matter much anymore that she hated me. It was time to turn my attention to a whole class full of first-grade girls. Mrs. Richards noticed me pointing around and ticking their names off on a scribbled list while we were supposed to be cutting out construction paper clover leaves or something. I had a crush on Mrs. Richards, too.

Cynthia Martinelli was no crush. We were in fourth grade by that time, and I spent most recess periods that year tagging along with her and her friends. She was pretty nice to me. A lot nicer than Holly Marshall, anyway. But, of course, I never tried to kiss her. That was the year I learned how to jump rope.

Jumping rope is not a talent that impresses fourth-grade boys. In fact, fourth-grade boys tend to say uncool things to other fourth-grade boys who hang around with girls. So if, in fourth grade, you happen to be the kind of guy who passes up kickball to jump rope with Cynthia Martinelli, you've got a problem. Guys don't take you very seriously. Girls don't, either. They just sort of put up with you. Which is the real reason I finally defected from the girls' side of the playground back to the guys'.

It was a good move, I think, because that's when I got to be friends with Andy and Matt. They were probably my first real friends, and they're still around. It's kind of hard to believe we've been buddies for so long. Maybe it's because of the way we got to know each other.

There I was, just beginning to get used to the way guys act around each other—mean. Being the only brother of three older sisters hadn't prepared me for all that, and spending so much time jumping rope certainly hadn't shed any light on the subject. So I was pretty shocked when I saw this one kid, Andrew Hanes, actually trying to strangle skinny little Matthew Forster. Andy was huge, even back then. He had these beady blue eyes that could freeze you stiff when he stared you down. That's what had happened to Matt. He'd done something or other that had made Andy mad (I never figured out what the heck it was) and was frozen stiff when Andy came over to collect on it. I could almost hear Matt's pint-sized bones rattling when he loosened up enough to shiver.

That didn't stop big bully Hanes, who had his victim down in about three seconds flat. I was pretty sure that Matt Forster was going to die, just for doing some stupid thing that had made Andy Hanes mad.

Before I knew what I was doing, I was running over to them and yelling, "Stop! Stop!" at the top of my lungs. All I remember thinking was that it wasn't going to work, that Matt was probably already paralyzed or something, and Andy wasn't going to listen to me, anyway. But later I found out that everyone on the whole playground listened to me. Bonita Jimenez told me, just a couple of years ago, in fact, that every face within about a quarter mile had turned to stare while I tried to save Matthew Forster's life. They still haven't forgotten it, after all these years. But that's another story.

The amazing thing was that Andy turned around, too. He still had his big, knotty hands around Matt's scrawny neck, but at least he wasn't throttling him anymore. He was just sort of sitting on Matt's stomach, pinning him to the concrete, and looking at me like I had gone crazy.

I had, I guess. It was panic that had made me run and scream. And panic that made me stop dead in my tracks when I got to within a couple of feet of Andy and saw the icy look in his eyes. I thought, *this is it. I'm next.*

But I wasn't. And Matt wasn't dead. He was laughing.

Sort of gurgling at first, on account of Andy's fingers still being on his jugular. Then I could see that he was actually laughing his own incredible laugh that I heard sometimes in class. Andy joined in, loud and rowdy.

I never heard the end of it. For the rest of the year, they'd stage these little murder scenes for my benefit. Murder in the cafeteria—knifing. Murder in the boy's room—drowning. Murder on the sidewalk—shootout.

It was bad.

How could I possibly have known that Andy hadn't really been planning to strangle Matt out there on the playground? It had sure looked like it, for cripes sake. And how could I possibly have known that the reason Andy and Matt kept bugging me was they were beginning to like me and wanted me to be one of their buddies? I guess they figured that any guy who would make such a fool of himself in front of the whole school would be great to have around, at least for laughs.

As different as the three of us were, we managed to become pretty tight. Andy, the big blond football jock. Matt, practically the smartest kid in school. And me, somewhere in between. We were the strangest combination anyone could have thrown together, but we got to know each other pretty well.

Except there was one thing Andy and Matt didn't know about me: my feelings concerning those "other" people in the world. Namely, girls. Just because I didn't hang out with them anymore didn't mean I had lost interest. My best friends had no idea that year after year I suffered through a whole string of secret loves. Because I kept my mouth shut about Nora Tyler and Dee Wilson and everyone else. No more blatant staring or smiling or *For Your Eyes Only* love notes. I'd learned my lesson.

Things changed some by the time we hit seventh grade. We

started talking a lot about girls—how they looked, mostly. And by our freshman year, each of us had even gone out on a few dates. I don't really know how Andy and Matt went from making fun of girls to appreciating them. But it happened. There was a month once when practically all I heard about from Andy was this Appearance Rating System he had worked out, and at one point Matt started developing insane crushes on older women.

But by the time we turned sixteen, they were still in a fantasy stage about females. For some reason they felt perfectly comfortable getting hooked on Bo Derek or Victoria Principal or Ms. Delacorte, our history teacher, but when it came to real live girls our own age, they kind of clammed up. Girls at school were filed away into categories like Boring, Ugly, or Stuck-up.

I couldn't sympathize. There were a lot of girls I really liked, just as regular people. But that didn't make a whole lot of sense to Andy and Matt. I even tried explaining it to them once, which was sticking my neck out pretty far. Especially since the kind of girls I felt best about were the ones most like my sisters —the independent, down-to-earth type—a type that Andy and Matt weren't interested in. All of which makes it even harder to understand how I fell for Julienne Kelsey.

The day it happened I was walking Mrs. Musil's dog through Webber Falls' one decent park, which isn't too far from my house. The dog was driving me nuts. A really small, disgusting Yorkie that I normally couldn't stand the sight of, it had little red bows tied into its fur and always barked in this sickeningly high voice at everything that passed Mrs. Musil's house. Sometimes it even ran out and tried to bite bike tires. Anyway, the only reason I had anything to do with that animal was that Mrs. Musil was paying me fairly big bucks to feed it and take it for walks while she was gone. That was one of my professions that year. And with most pets, I enjoyed it. I had little cards made up and everything. *Peter Garroway: Vacation Pet Caretaker.*

So there I was, Vacation Pet Caretaking, while MacArthur, the little squirt, was snuffling through the bushes and fallen leaves. He'd stop to snuffle for a while, break off into a bullet-speed trot, then stop dead in his tiny tracks again. And the whole time, I never let go of his leash. I knew better than that.

His hour was almost up, so I was tugging on the leash, trying to lead him home, when he found this pile of trash in the hollow of an enormous old oak tree. If there's one thing dogs love, it's trash. Especially small dogs. They're nuts about getting their noses all dirty and sticky, then having to sneeze to get the germs out. The last thing I wanted was for him to get into something gross and get sick, so I was behind the tree with him, trying to yank him away without breaking his worthless neck.

That was when I heard it. The thunder of hooves. At first, I thought it might be the rumble of a truck on the highway or something, but when I poked my head out from behind the tree, I saw the galloping horse. And the galloping horse saw me. And so did the person riding it.

Everything happened pretty fast. But I had time to think about how they all matched: the horse, the fallen leaves, and the rider. They all seemed to be the same color. Rusty reds and oranges on the ground, toasted brown on the horse, and somewhere between cinnamon and caramel in the girl's streaming long hair. For an instant, I even saw her face—all flushed from the ride. She looked wild, kind of, and free.

Then MacArthur ruined it all. He dashed out like a little weasel, nearly hanging himself on his collar and scaring the daylights out of the horse.

It reared up on its hind legs and belted out this horrible,

6

upset noise that only a horse can make. That, in turn, scared the daylights out of MacArthur, who practically jumped into my arms.

But only temporarily. As soon as the girl got the horse under control, MacArthur was squirming around and yipping and yapping again.

It was then that I realized who the girl was. The reason I didn't recognize her sooner was that she had looked so different while the horse was galloping. Beautiful, in fact. Now her face had gone pale and her eyes had gotten wide and scared-looking, just the way they always were at school.

A lot was going through my head at that point. For one thing, I was amazed by the fact that I was thinking of Julienne Kelsey as beautiful. For another, I was trying to figure out a way to keep MacArthur quiet. He was wiggling all over, and it was impossible to clamp his mouth shut. I felt ridiculous. Finally, while those huge eyes of Julienne's stared down at us, I remembered what Mrs. Musil had mentioned about rubbing MacArthur's belly. It worked. His irritating barks turned into muffled little yelps.

At the same time, I was also thinking about how frightened Julienne looked, and how that was making me want to apologize, even though she and her horse had no business being that far off the horse trail in the first place.

It must have been that expression on her face, along with the memory of how she had looked a few moments earlier that made me stutter instead of talk. I think I said something like, "Sorry. Hope you're O.K." But whatever it was didn't seem to matter much. Suddenly, without any warning, Julienne kind of half-smiled. It was more of a smile than anything I'd ever seen on her face. Then, with just a tiny flick of her wrist and turn of her heel, she communicated something to the horse. And, in another moment, she had cantered away from me and MacArthur.

I knew it was a canter because one of my sisters was once very into horses. That's also how I knew that Julienne looked pretty good on a horse. By equestrian standards, that is. Not to mention my own.

Chapter Two

I knew I was going to ask her out. There was no doubt about that, even though I wasn't at all sure about why I wanted to.

Groggily, I stared into the bathroom mirror Monday morning and imagined what Julienne would look like standing beside me. There I'd be, six feet tall in my bare feet, with hair somewhere between light brown and dark blond, and eyes somewhere between green and blue. There she'd be, coming just barely up to my shoulder, with that cinnamony-caramel silky hair and those big brown eyes. Her skin would be creamy and pale, and her mouth would be set in that half-scared straight line. I, on the other hand, still had some tan left over from the summer and had a funny-looking dimple right in the middle of my chin. Thanks to working out at the racquetball club with my dad, I was in fairly good shape and could bench-press two hundred and ten pounds. Julienne looked like she weighed about a third that much. It didn't seem that we'd make the best-matched pair around.

Even aside from looks, we had hardly anything in common. Julienne was quiet and kept to herself. I rarely stop talking and like to have people around. According to Andy, who had Julienne in his English class, she wrote the best papers in there and was always reading. I, on the contrary, wasn't too nuts about English. The grammar part had turned me off a long time ago. And Matt said that Julienne had to be the only person at Frazier capable of flunking out of Mr. Hoff's trigonometry. That's my best subject. So why, I wondered while buttoning on a flannel shirt, was I thinking about asking Julienne Kelsey to go out with me? She was nothing at all like the girls I'd dated before.

Running a comb over my head, I decided that Julienne was different, all right. She was so different that my friends had both mentioned her before, although they pretty much ignored girls who weren't super-gorgeous. Matt and Andy both thought Julienne was strange. But she seemed kind of mysterious to me.

On my way downstairs, I frowned. Because now that I knew *why* I was going to ask Julienne out, I had a second question. *How?*

"Well, well. Good morning, trooper. You're just in time for Dad's blueberry bran muffins." My sister Colleen was, as usual, bright and cheery as a canary.

"You're up early today, Peter," my dad observed, pouring his coffee.

"Glad you could make it," Mom chimed in.

Being a serious sleeper, I wasn't too surprised by the comments. Usually, I got up just in time to spend a few minutes with them at breakfast, our only meal together. You'd think that with both parents working at home on their own business, a family would see more of each other. Instead, Garroway Computer Software kept us about fifteen times busier than we'd been back in the days when Mom and Dad worked at outside jobs.

Just as I finished breakfast, Colleen gave us the latest news about her job hunt. Now that she was through with college, she was helping out part-time at home between interviews.

"On Wednesday through Friday I won't be here to answer the phones, folks. That personnel agency Suzanne recommended got me a few prospects."

"That's wonderful, Colleen," Mom said over her cup of coffee. "Will that work out O.K. with you, Peter?"

"Sure," I answered stoically, not adding that I wouldn't mind the extra pay, even at my parents' minimum-wage, slave-labor rates.

Walking to school, I passed Carol Sawyer, a girl I used to date, and her bunch of friends. I waved, but she just smiled and kept talking to them. My thoughts went back to Julienne, who didn't seem to have any friends at all, except for a couple of kids I saw her sitting with sometimes at lunch. One of them was Blair Doran, a girl who won practically every important part in the school plays. The other was Blair's boyfriend, Stephen Belsaw. Andy had almost gotten into a fight with Stephen once after calling Blair flaky. So I didn't think I stood much chance of working my way to Julienne through them. I'd have to do it on my own.

My chance came sooner than I could have hoped—first period. Julienne's class turned out to be right next to mine, a fact that my habit of getting there mere seconds before the bell rang had kept me from noticing before. But that day I was early. And just before I went in, I saw her.

She was rushing into her classroom. It was just luck that made her look my way. Her pretty brown eyes widened so far I thought maybe I had blueberry muffin crumbs all over me.

11

Resisting the urge to find out, I tried to look friendly. Against all odds, I smiled.

"Hi, again." Normally I might have thought up something more charming and brilliant to say to a girl, but this girl looked like she wanted to get away as soon as possible and that froze the words in my throat. I just kept smiling.

It didn't help. She was getting ready to bolt. So I got myself out of her sight and into the classroom.

It bothered me all morning. What was wrong? Had MacArthur's attempted attack on her horse really messed up her ride that badly? Or was I just not her type?

As lunchtime approached and I got hungry, my theories got even more depressing. Maybe Julienne had a secret life outside of school that included a boyfriend—some incredibly smooth and cool dude of a guy who really knew how to talk to sophisticated women and never flubbed up. She was devoted to him, of course, and when she smiled, she was just laughing at me.

So why should I keep banging my head against the wall?

The question was answered at lunchtime.

"Hey, Garroway, sit yourself down," Andy suggested with a convincing yank on my arm. I'd been standing beside the table, nonchalantly radaring the room for Ms. J.K.

"It makes him nervous to have people just stand around and watch him make a pig of himself," Matt told me. "Didn't you know that?"

"Yeah," I said, beginning to feel better. If nothing else, Matt and Andy were a known quantity. Familiar. "Guess I do." I sat down and tuned into their talk.

Meanwhile, I was forgetting to watch for Julienne. And that was why I didn't think twice about it when the three of us went over to the water fountain for a drink. As usual, Andy elbowed his way to be first in line, but Matt poked a finger into just the right spot between Andy's fifth and sixth ribs, making him double over with tickled torture. Taking my chance, I went for the water, only to have Andy grab my shoulders and pull with all his might.

We were all fairly positive that eventually some teacher or other was going to come over and give us a hard time about "horseplay in the cafeteria." But it was one of our time-honored traditions, worthy of the risk. Although, personally, I was hoping we'd outgrow it soon and move on to something else.

I was in a good mood, though, still nudging at my friends, when we turned to go. And there she was, sitting at the table just beside us, smiling enough to make that delicate porcelain-and-ivory face of hers crack.

Chapter Three

I hardly even considered smiling back.

Number one, I was too shocked. And number two, I was very aware of Matt and Andy standing next to me. Whenever they saw me so much as nod to a girl, they hassled me for days. And with Julienne, I knew I'd *never* hear the end of it.

So I walked on, forcing myself to concentrate on one thing: *She doesn't exist.*

I spent the whole afternoon trying to forgive myself. How could I have been such a Class-A, premium-grade wimp? Julienne Kelsey had smiled at me. Nicely. And just because I'd been worried about my socially retarded, bimbo friends, I had ignored her.

My only consolation was telling myself that it wouldn't happen again. In fact, I was determined to make up for it as soon as possible, which turned out to be right after school. I plotted out my strategy during sixth-period study hall. Knowing that Julienne had math with Matt last period, I decided that I'd have to stake myself out a couple of doors down the hall and wait for her to come out. Doing so meant that I'd have to be on my toes, ready to leap out of my desk in history class and make a dash for it as soon as the seventh-period end bell rang. Then I'd have to run down the hall, up the stairs, and back down another hall, all the while hoping desperately for two things. One, that Julienne was slow, and two, that Matt cleared out before her.

All through history, I was prepared. The problem was that Mr. Lloyd wasn't. He put off giving us our assignment until the bell rang. I couldn't very well just jump up in the middle of it, so I mentally bound myself to the chair and waited. Which, of course, caused me to be too late.

By the time I made it up to the second floor, the first person I recognized was Matt. And he, unfortunately, saw me. As he walked up, I kept my eyes on the Room 241 doorway.

"What are *you* doing here, Pete? Don't you have Lloyd's class downstairs seventh period?" He pulled out an oversized handkerchief to blow his nose. Matt suffered from about a dozen different allergies.

"Um, yeah. But I have to, um . . . go to the library. See ya."

As casually as possible, I walked away from him, then stopped about ten feet down to look back. He was going into the stairwell.

There was one advantage to this game, I thought, as I searched the hall for Julienne. Feeling like a secret agent could be fun. But I didn't see her anywhere. This secret agent had just failed in his mission and was wondering if he'd get up the nerve to try it again tomorrow.

15

That was when I saw the flash of reddish-brown, just about to disappear around the corner. It was her!

My first impulse was to run after her. Once I had her in sight, though, all my doubts were returning, as I watched her long hair swing from side to side behind her as she walked. Maybe Matt thought she was strange, but she seemed more sophisticated and mysterious than any other teenage girl I knew. What the heck was I going to say to her?

From a few yards back, watching her get books out of her locker near the chem lab, I decided. I'd just say, "Hi," and "How you doing?" and "Sure am glad I don't have MacArthur with me today," or something like that. Then I'd ask her to join me for a Coke at The Snax. It was no big deal. After all, she'd smiled at me, hadn't she? Completely on her own, she'd given me that big, beautiful smile.

"Um, excuse me. Julienne?"

I was right behind her when I said her name. She had just started to walk away from her locker, and her canvas bag was bulging with books. I didn't think she'd heard. So I said it again, louder.

"Julienne?"

This time I was positive she heard, because with all the force of a tornado, she whirled around to look at me. The reason it seemed like a tornado was that her book bag went flying out of her hands, and every single one of the books came crashing out onto the floor. It was loud.

In the next second I was down on my hands and knees, picking up the books and putting them back into her bag. Maybe, I remember thinking insanely, if I put them all back fast enough she'd forget it ever happened. Maybe she'd forget it had been me who had (1) made her horse go wild, (2) ignored her when she smiled, and (3) sneaked up and startled the heck out of her right in the middle of Frazier High.

My mouth had already started moving. It was moving so

16

fast, in fact, that I almost didn't notice one of the books I was putting back into her bag. With a title like *Raging Tide of Passion* and a cover showing a man kissing a woman whose dress was about to fall off, it wasn't a book I'd normally just glance over. But at that moment all I did was make a sort of subconscious mental note of it.

"Here you go," I said as I handed the full bag to her. "Sorry I startled you."

I figured it would be a good idea to smile again. I tried to look as friendly and apologetic as possible.

It must not have been enough. All she did was stare back at me, as if I were a six-foot baboon on the loose.

Automatically, I started talking.

"Well." After that it all came gushing out. "I thought maybe, that is, I was hoping you'd like to come with me to The Snax for a Coke or something, just to sort of make up for causing you all that trouble in the park a couple of days ago . . ." I took a breath. "You have time?"

Already, several possible answers started ringing in my brain, to prepare for what she might actually say. *I can't,* she'd yawn. *My boyfriend would process you through his Cuisinart.* Or, *I happen to be running late for my private dance lesson with Rudolf Nureyev. Would you please step out of my way?*

When her answer finally came, however, it was nothing like that. It was a hundred times worse. One, single, devastating:

"No."

No? I wanted to ask. Just *no?*

But then she mumbled something about being sorry and about having to get home. That was all I needed.

"Oh, well, then how about if I walk you? Partway, that is?"

She looked surprised. So was I, over the fact that I was sticking my neck out this far.

17

"I'll just walk with you up to the corner," I persisted. "How about that? It won't make you late. I promise."

She seemed to consider it for a minute, then nodded. It was all I could do not to pick her up and *carry* her to the corner.

Instead, I started talking.

I honestly don't know exactly what I said. It had something to do with family responsibilities, and how I knew what it was like to have to rush home after school, and all kinds of other stuff she didn't seem the least bit interested in, because she didn't say a word. But it kept me calm. Talking is one thing that runs in my family. None of us ever clams up. We talk no matter what.

That was just what it seemed I was doing at the time. Because for a flicker of an instant, just as we reached the corner, I thought I saw Julienne's lips turn up. Just a little. A Mona Lisa smile. I could almost hear her talking to her boyfriend.

Oh, Charles, darling! You should have seen this absolute clown of a boy slobbering after me today—

"Well," I said quickly. "This is the corner. See ya." And I zoomed off across the street.

Chapter Four

There was Pioneer Beef Stew for lunch the next day at school. It was definitely the most disgusting, supposedly edible stuff ever created by the Webber Falls Independent School District cafeteria. And it was a perfect match for the way I felt. Rotten.

Sitting there with Andy and Matt, I was picking around the chunks of unrecognizable substances on my tray, wishing that horrible things would happen to MacArthur the dog. This whole Julienne business was his fault. If he had just behaved himself like a good little worthless lapdog, I would never have seen Julienne look so beautiful on the horse. Those little stirrings of curiosity I'd had about her before that afternoon in the park would never have amounted to anything.

While I found a couple of potato morsels to put in my mouth, I was also wishing that I hadn't put off packing my lunch last night. There hadn't been time this morning, so now

19

I was stuck with this greenish-gray muck. And that was just the topic that good ol' Andy picked to discuss.

"Didn't bring your own lunch today, eh?"

I didn't look up. "You're brilliant sometimes, Andy."

"Just thought I'd mention it. Looks like you need a little sympathy for having to eat that stuff. How 'bout some of this sandwich? Here, take half. I'm not so crazy about chicken salad, anyway."

He was practically shoving it in my face. Andy might have had a heart of gold, but sometimes he didn't know when to stop.

"Come on, take it."

"You're a growing boy," I said, pushing it away. "Eat it yourself. Thanks, anyway."

"All right. Starve yourself." Andy shrugged and bit off a huge chunk. "Don't know why my mom gives me *two* chicken salads."

I knew I shouldn't say it, but I was feeling so down that day that the words just came flying out of my mouth. "At least she gives you *something*." Now the door was wide open.

Matt picked up on it first. "Ah, the joys of working mothers . . ."

As usual, I wanted to put my fist down his throat. But I had to just grit my teeth and get through Session No. 1,672 of Matt and Andy's continuing commentary on nontraditional family life.

"Yeah," Andy mumbled between gulps of milk. "I'd go *nuts* if my mom worked."

It did no good to remind them that cooking, cleaning, shopping, and chauffering *were* work. I'd tried telling them before. Maybe someday they'd stop thinking that all families had to be just like theirs—with the dad working at an outside job and the mom at home.

20

Luckily, the talk turned to Conquest, a board game the three of us had been playing every Saturday for a long time. Either they knew I could outtalk them in a debate on the mom topic, or they sensed that I wasn't feeling so great. Neither of them is the kind of guy who'll hit you when you're down. I mean, we all razzed each other a lot, but when it came down to it, we were buddies. Buddies who had stuck together a long, long time.

"What would you get if Batman and Robin got run over by a truck?" Andy was asking Don, another friend of ours who had just sat down.

"Uh, let's see. Wait a minute, I've heard this one, and it's pretty stupid. But I don't remem—"

"Flatman and Ribbon."

Andy could never hold back a punch line, no matter how corny. Don started nudging me.

"Your turn, Garroway."

"O.K. O.K. What's the difference between a boxer and a man with a cold?"

They were all watching me and grinning. I could tell none of them had ever heard this one before.

"O.K., we give up," Andy urged.

"The boxer knows his blows, and the man—"

The words caught in my throat. I felt like someone was strangling me.

"Yeah? And the man what?" Andy was asking.

I couldn't see any of them. Andy and Matt and Don had disappeared. The only thing I could see was standing just a few feet away from our table, behind my friends' backs. Julienne. Smiling.

"Hey, he's choking!"

I was. As soon as I'd torn my eyes away from Julienne, I had felt something prickle up and down my throat and make me red in the face.

Andy got up and started whomping me on the back.

"I told you you should have eaten my sandwich! This stuff is enough to kill you!"

Matt was beside him in a second, trying to haul him off me. "Don't hit him! That's not what you do with a choking victim!"

I had to wait a minute before telling them I was really O.K. Because when I looked back up, Julienne was gone.

Chapter Five

I stood exactly seven paces away from her locker, trying to picture the life-size poster of Humphrey Bogart I'd seen in a shop in the city. That was exactly how I wanted to look, minus the cigarette.

Meanwhile, just about everyone I knew in the whole school walked by. Andy stopped to ask me if I was feeling O.K. now, and Matt looked me over carefully, then told me he'd get together with me tomorrow night if I needed some help with the chemistry problems. I was half-afraid that they'd get curious about what I was doing, just standing there. Maybe they'd get it into their heads to hide down the hall somewhere and spy on me in case I started choking again. It must be obvious that I had been out of it lately. But it looked like neither of them was really out to bug me, and they both had activities after school that day, anyway.

Then Juanita Marlowe, of all people, stopped to talk to me.

Less than a week ago, I'd have flipped out if she'd done that. With her wavy black hair, sexy green eyes, and terrific other things, I normally would have had my eyes glued to her. Today, my eyes roamed all over the hall.

"Well, I just wanted to say hi," she said as she walked away.

Suddenly I realized that I hadn't been listening to a word she'd said. She could have been begging me to kiss her, for all I knew.

I didn't care. I was relieved to see her go. And she had left not a moment too soon. Because Julienne Kelsey was coming down the hall.

I watched her approach, but she didn't seem to see me at all. Her long hair fell around her shoulders like a veil. It seemed to spread this mysterious glow around her, as if she knew a million things that none of the rest of us did. And her eyes . . . As she got closer I saw them staring straight ahead, far away into some secret.

I wanted to get her attention right away, so that I wouldn't startle her again. But when I moved away from the lockers and fell into step with her, she hardly blinked.

After she opened her locker door, I hung onto it for support. It was as if the whole smile thing in the cafeteria had never happened. Maybe I had imagined it. She wouldn't even look at me now. If I didn't jump in soon, I'd lose my nerve.

"Well. How do you feel about my walking you home today?"

She turned toward me right away. "Today?"

I knew she was going to laugh.

"Well, yeah. If you're not busy or anything." My voice had lowered to a mumble. Maybe I could pretend later that I hadn't really done any of this. But before I could look away, she nodded.

That must mean yes, I thought. *Yes!*

"Well, um . . . great." My voice was returning. "Which way do we go?"

She pointed in the direction of my own neighborhood. As we walked along, I babbled out some clumsy apology for MacArthur's having scared her horse in the park. I thought I'd better put out a good reason for this big production of wanting to walk her home, just in case she decided to tell me about her boyfriend or her general disinterest in total duds like me.

But she didn't say anything like that. In fact, she was laughing. Not a ridiculing laugh, but a friendly kind. Girls, I knew from the experience of having three sisters, do not laugh that way when they are making fun of you.

"You didn't cause me any trouble at all, Peter. That horse is way too excitable. She spooks at everything."

Excitable. Julienne Kelsey was finally talking to me!

It was enough to make me speechless. Which doesn't happen often. For at least a whole minute, I found myself unable to go beyond clever one-word replies like, "Really?"

"As a matter of fact," she was saying, "it was good for me. It made the ride more . . . interesting."

Everything from her tone of voice to her smile let me know that she was not about to tell me about her Richard Gere type boyfriend.

"Well," I said finally. "I'm glad to hear you don't hate me." It came out sounding more direct than I had wanted it to. Sticking my neck out was becoming a habit. And once I got started . . . "You know what? Up there on your horse, Julienne, you looked great. It seemed like you had no doubts at all about what to do when your horse jumped up like that. I mean, if it had been me . . ." I shook my head. "Horses don't like me too much."

"Oh?" she said, leaning her head to one side and grinning.

25

I could feel that velvety brown gaze on me. "You look like you could handle just about anything, Peter."

Thus time I didn't go speechless. True to family tradition, I started talking up a storm. A storm that I hoped would cloud over the fact that I was near collapse. There was no mistaking her tone of voice this time. I was willing to bet my big toe on it.

Julienne Kelsey was flirting.

As we neared a row of nice-looking townhouses, I tried to move that head-spinning thought aside so that I could do some serious thinking. And talking. Movies was the subject that rolled off my tongue.

"My friends and I saw this one flick—you probably heard about it, even though it wasn't very popular here—*Fly by Night*. It was kind of a science fiction thriller type of thing, but not real spooky or gross. Um, do you like movies like that?"

She nodded. For a second, I worried that I was losing her interest. She really hadn't put in much whenever I'd asked her questions. But I kept going.

"They've got this sequel out now, *Fly by Day*. I've heard it's pretty good. Are you interested, maybe for this Saturday night?"

Again, she nodded. She wasn't one to waste her breath, I figured. But it *was* a nod, and that did mean yes.

I could have jumped off her doorstep and done a cartwheel right across her front lawn. Instead, I stood rooted to my spot facing her and looked straight into her eyes. Which was a mistake, because now what I wanted to do was kiss her, barely half an hour after I'd even gotten her to *talk* to me.

One of my hands reached out and sort of rested, for three seconds, on her shoulder. It was the kind of friendly pat you'd give your mother. Right after that, I started to back away.

26

"Glad we had a chance to talk, Julienne. And I, um . . . I'll be in touch about the movie Saturday night, O.K.? I'll look for you at school when I find out the times for it. O.K.? See you."

Before she could change her mind and bring Richard Gere out of the house, I leapt off the little porch and headed home.

Chapter Six

It wasn't going to matter how much they'd hoot and holler. I was going to tell Matt and Andy about Julienne. They'd get used to it. Shouldn't they be happy that I was happy? And if they weren't, were they really friends?

I didn't get to find out that day, because it was Thursday, one of the days I had to go home for lunch and answer the phones for Garroway Computer Software. After school I came right home to do some envelope-stuffing, and I barely had time to get my homework done that night before dropping into bed. There was no time to even think about calling anybody.

I had to put my plan on hold until the next morning, when Andy was supposed to give me a ride to school. His car appeared in front of my house at the incredibly early hour of 6:55 A.M. To please my parents, he didn't honk, but he did come up and bang on our front door. I awoke to the sound of his voice thundering good mornings to my family.

Andy was going to owe me something for this one, I figured. Because he had ruined my plan for talking to him about Julienne. The last thing I felt like doing so early in the morning was launching into a confession. I was going to do it sometime soon, though, and when I did, I wasn't going to take any flak from Andy over it.

"You know why I picked you up early today, don't you?" he asked as we got into his car.

I yawned. "No idea."

"Delacorte."

"Ms. Delacorte?" I was starting to wake up.

"Who else, fleabrain? I promised Matt I'd go with him to that yearbook staff breakfast she's putting on to bring in new volunteers."

"Huh?" I screwed up my face at him. "Matt doesn't have the slightest interest in even *looking* at the yearbook, much less—"

"Not the yearbook. *Delacorte*. She's the one he's going to look at."

I groaned. "Not that again. I thought he was off that kick."

"Hah! He hasn't gotten off the Miss Belinda Delacorte kick since he had her for Western Civilization in ninth grade. Come on, you've got to remember how he jacked his schedule around this year so he'd have her for American history." Andy shook his head knowingly. "He'll do anything to get near that broad."

"Woman."

"Huh?"

"Woman," I repeated. "The Atlantic is broad, the Great Plains are broad, but Ms. Dela—"

"All right, all right. I get the point." He turned into the

29

school parking lot. "Just wanted to make sure you were prepared to watch him puppydog around after her during this breakfast thing." He shook his head again. "Man. The things I do for friendship. And I bet all they'll have is juice and donuts."

That *was* all they had at the gathering in the cafeteria. Andy was right about another thing, too. Matt acted *exactly* like a puppydog around Ms. Delacorte. He followed her with those sad gray eyes of his all over the room. It was as if his attention were led around on a leash by her tall, centerfold-quality body. Seeing the normally cool, reserved Matt in such a state was a shock.

Did he really expect Delacorte to say, "Oh yes, Matthew, my love. I'm yours. Only, perhaps we should wait until you graduate." I mean, what could a sixteen-year-old kid with braces on his teeth hope for from a twenty-six-year-old knockout? He was in for some killer heartbreak.

That was what I tried to tell him as we left the cafeteria. I felt like shaking him. But I held back. He needed careful deprogramming.

"Um, you know, Matt. There are some pretty interesting girls in this school."

"I know." He was still grinning.

"You do?"

"Of course," he said, looking at me as if *I* were the space cadet. "Why do you think I went to that breakfast?"

I searched his face, and found *Delacorte* written all over it. There had to be a way to get through to him.

By the time I got going toward my class, I was still feeling muddled and groggy. Too many weird things were happening. And I had yet to tell anyone about Julienne.

Julienne!

The first thing I thought of when I saw her waiting outside my first-period classroom was that I had forgotten all about looking up the showtimes for *Fly by Day*, which had to be what she was waiting to see me for. I was all ready to avoid the issue by laughing over the fact that we were both hopelessly late for class, when suddenly she spoke up.

"Peter? I wanted to . . . talk."

Talk? Of course we could talk, I thought. About anything. I was totally open to any topic of conversation. Until, that is, I saw how serious she looked. Whatever she had in mind didn't seem to be something I wanted to hear.

But I agreed to meet her at her locker after school. I couldn't see her before then, since I had to have lunch at home again today.

I practiced my speech all day. *Listen, Julienne. It's really O.K. that you have this boyfriend who wants to beat me to a pulp for asking you out. We'll just be adults about it while you clear that mess up. Dump him. Get him out of the way. No problem. I'm sure he's mature and sensible.*

I didn't get a chance to use a word of it as we walked toward our neighborhood that afternoon. What she wanted to talk about had nothing at all to do with a boyfriend. As far as I could tell.

"I'm afraid I've made a mistake," she began, tossing her hair over her shoulder. "Saturday night—"

That was the part that threw me.

"—my mother's friends are opening an art exhibit at the Village Gallery in town. I'd forgotten all about it when you asked me out." She looked straight at me, and I could tell she wasn't lying. "You see, I can't miss it, Peter."

It was understandable. Of course. An art show. Something she'd promised her mother. I'd never felt so relieved. It wasn't a boyfriend. An art show I could compete with.

She spoke. "I was wondering—"

Without meaning to, I cut her off. "We could go another night."

31

"Another . . . ?" She looked annoyed. "Oh, sure," she said with a definite lack of enthusiasm. "Another night. But—"

"It doesn't have to be this week. Next weekend would be O.K." I knew I was overdoing it. Why couldn't I just be calm and slick and keep my mouth shut?

"Next Saturday? All right."

Before I could enjoy another wave of relief, she added, "But there's still the question of—"

My heart stumbled and stopped dead.

"—whether or not you'd be interested in going to the art show with me. It must sound terribly dull, but really—"

"An art show?" I was amazed. Julienne Kelsey, Sophisticated Ex-City Girl, was inviting Peter Garroway, Country Clod, to her mother's friends' art show. She wasn't ashamed of me. She thought I could fit into her world. I wanted to swing her into my arms and dance down the sidewalk. But through sheer willpower, I kept my voice low and even. "Sure. I'd like that." Only my smile came bursting through.

And that was when I looked around and noticed that we were standing right in front of my house. I felt like a real clown. Somehow, I must have absentmindedly guided us there instead of to her house. The back of my brain must have been reminding me of the fact that I had to get home and stuff envelopes.

At first I felt like apologizing. Girls walking guys home wasn't exactly standard practice around Webber Falls. But then, an echo of what Colleen would probably have to say about it came into my head.

It's good for girls to feel independent, and to get used to taking care of themselves.

"Seven o'clock?" Julienne was saying.

I nodded. "Seven o'clock." And then another voice popped

32

into my head. Matt's. *Seven o'clock, guys, for Conquest on Saturday.*

"Saturday," I murmured aloud.

When I'd finally pulled myself together, she was staring up at me. "Well, I've got to go in now," I said apologetically. "It's my afternoon to stuff envelopes."

"I see," was all she said.

But she couldn't see what was racing through my mind. After I said goodbye and started up the path, a very clear image presented itself to me. Matt and Andy, coming to my house toting a big, heavy rope and looking for a solid tree.

Chapter Seven

All I had to do was tell them I couldn't make it. They could play Conquest without me, for just this one Saturday.

But I knew it wouldn't be that easy. Saturday Conquest had been a habit with us for so long—part of being buddies. Of course, we couldn't go on playing every Saturday forever. But I'd have to come up with a good reason for backing out the first time. And I doubted if Andy and Matt would consider a girl a good enough reason. Especially not a girl like Julienne.

I hadn't had a chance to tell them anything about Julienne yet. How could I suddenly spring it on them, adding the minor detail that I was skipping the game to be with her? That was definitely not the best way to get Matt Forster and Andy Hanes, Friends, used to the idea of Julienne Kelsey, Girlfriend. Especially since she was the Julienne Kelsey they referred to as "strange." Breaking it to them was going to have to be done more carefully.

I thought about it all Friday morning, before hearing my mother's remark during lunch about Colleen's birthday the next day.

The wheels in my head were set in motion. Colleen's birthday. The perfect excuse.

That night I called the Game Master, Matt.

"Hullo, Pete. Are you working on the chemistry assignment?"

Just like Matt, I thought. Business first.

"No, I finished it. I've been trudging through this battle-by-battle account of the Civil War for a quiz in Lloyd's class."

"Fort Sumter, April fifteenth, eighteen six—"

"Thanks, Matt. I'm convinced you know it backwards and forwards. You don't have to recite the whole thing."

"I did for Ms. Delacorte."

I sighed in exasperation. "Good for you. But that's not what I called about. It's about Saturday night."

"Yes?"

"You know, the Conquest session." I was stalling.

"Seven o'clock, at my house," he said. "We agreed not to play in the afternoon on account of Andy's football practice."

"I know that. The thing is that I, um . . . see, there's a problem. I'm afraid I've made a mistake." Julienne's words were coming in handy. "My sister's birthday is tomorrow, Saturday night."

"Saturday night is her birthday? What about the rest of the day?"

"You know what I mean. We're celebrating it tomorrow night. See, I'd forgotten all about it. And I can't miss it. I'm committed."

"You should be."

"Huh?"

"Committed. To an institution. You're nuts if you think we're going to let you off this easy. We already switched it from the afternoon. It was your idea!"

I swallowed. Here it came—trouble. I was probably going to have to provide written proof of where exactly I'd be if not in his living room on Saturday night.

He continued. "Since it's a conflict with family plans, we'll allow you this one absence, oh lowly one. But it's going on your record. You should know."

I could tell he was only half-kidding. *Oh, grow up, Matt,* I thought. But I didn't say anything.

I called Andy, and after just a little more verbal abuse than I'd gotten from Matt, the matter was settled. I was off the hook.

It was the perfect alibi. Saturday night they'd both be at Matt's house, way over in the Oakmont neighborhood. There'd be no chance of their seeing us go into the art gallery. They never hung around in the ritzy Village area of downtown, anyway. In fact, no one from school did. So I'd be safe. And everything was working out perfectly A-okay for my date with Julienne.

When Saturday night came, however, I wasn't so sure. First of all, I had no idea what I was supposed to wear. I had never been to an art gallery in my life, let alone to an art show opening. What I imagined was some chandeliered room with champagne fountains, tuxedos, and designer gowns all over the place.

By the time I got to Julienne's house, though, just a few seconds before the digits on my watch blipped seven, I was feeling pretty good about the way I looked in my one decent sport coat and dress cords. But I was completely in the fog about how I was supposed to act. As far as manners went, I was a clown. In my family, we were all expected to be considerate and help each other out. But no one got any special favors. Not even me, after I got old enough to take care of myself. So I wasn't a fanatic about rushing to open doors for girls and things like that. I was never quite sure about when to say, "Allow me, madame," or "May I throw my coat over this puddle for you?" What if Julienne and this ultrasophisticated, artsy mother of hers expected all of that?

A smallish, smiling woman with hair the color of Julienne's threw open the door. She could have passed for about twenty-one.

"Well, hi! You must be Peter."

"Um, yes. I'm Peter Garroway."

"Good to meet you, Peter. And come on in. I'm Julienne's mother, Audrey Kelsey."

She put out her hand. Was I supposed to kiss it, the way Andy sometimes did to impress girls? Instead, I just shook it a little and nodded, surprised by her firm grip.

"I'm glad you could come to the exhibit tonight, Peter," she said while ushering me into a warm-looking living room. "We've all been looking forward to this opening, and I was happy that Julienne found someone who was brave enough to share it with us."

She grinned. Even though they were light blue, her eyes looked just like Julienne's for a second. Sort of slanted up a little at the corners and fringed with long, dark lashes. A lot of my worries about tonight went away.

When Julienne came down the stairs about five minutes later, it was exactly like a scene from an old movie. There should have been music playing in the background. Because she looked gorgeous. She came sweeping down those stairs with her hair all piled up on top of her head and little curls hanging down around the edges. She wore a silky kind of dress that looked great on her, and she had that mysterious, faraway look in her eyes.

On our way to the gallery, I could hardly pay attention to the road. I wanted to stare into her eyes and put my arms around her. Instead, I talked. That way, I managed to keep my head straight.

"I'm probably going to need some explanations about what's what tonight, Julienne. I'm a real dunce when it comes to art."

Out of the corner of my eye, I saw her smile. "Oh, it's not that hard to understand."

"How about a few pointers, then?"

"Well," she began. "At first, I suppose, abstract art—what we'll see tonight—can be overwhelming. All the colors and strange shapes and different styles can throw you off sometimes. They do me, anyway."

"They do?" Never having heard her say so much in one breath, I was amazed. Maybe she finally found me worth talking to.

At the gallery, she opened up even more. "See, this mural is an example of what we were talking about in the car. It doesn't make much sense right away. But just let it sink in for a while."

I tried, in spite of all the distractions around me. There were no chandeliers or champagne fountains, and people were dressed in everything from tuxedos and sequins to patched jeans and T-shirts.

"The artist isn't necessarily trying to say any one particular thing or show any one image," Julienne was saying. "I think she's trying to make you *feel* something."

A grin crept up on me. Being with Julienne was what I was feeling.

I can't say I understood everything that she, her mother, and their artist friends tried to explain that night. But I didn't feel anything like Peter Garroway, High School Kid. The paintings and sculptures did start to say something to me.

What they were saying, I wasn't exactly sure, but I had this terrific feeling that a whole new world was opening up to me. And so was Julienne.

Maybe it was because we were in the kind of atmosphere she felt comfortable in, with people she had known since she was little. I can't say for sure. But whatever it was, every now and then I caught a sparkle in her eyes, which made me pretty happy.

Until, that is, about ten o'clock, when one of the worst possible things I could have imagined actually happened. Two people I knew came up to us. Kids. Frazier High kids.

Chapter Eight

"Well, look who's here." Blair Doran walked up to Julienne and grabbed her elbow, all the while staring at me.

"So you got dragged into this, too, Garroway?" Stephen asked.

At first I kept quiet. Maybe I could pretend that I was having a terrible time, and that I really had gotten dragged into coming to the exhibit, so that later, I could make up some story to Matt and Andy about just why I had ended up here instead of at Colleen's imaginary birthday party.

Julienne was out in the middle of the street, I could say, *begging passersby for a ride*. Or, *She called me at the last minute, desperate for a date. Could I refuse?*

I made myself stop. How could I even consider doing anything like that, after the great time I'd been having with Julienne?

The four of us ended up going out for Chinese food. And it

turned out that Blair's mom was one of Julienne's mom's artsy friends. She and Stephen were not, therefore, spies for my Dastardly Duo.

In spite of all the stuffed mushrooms and lobster people had been giving us all night, my stomach was grumbling. Art appreciation took energy. I wolfed down three orders of egg rolls and a plate of chop suey.

Afterwards, when Blair and Stephen took off for their car, they left Julienne and me standing alone together on the sidewalk. I swear I didn't think twice about picking up her hand and holding it. And it felt right. She didn't flinch or tense up. Julienne was holding my hand as if it was nothing at all out of the ordinary.

"It's beautiful out here," she said.

I tried to answer. Julienne was practically the only living being capable of getting me tongue-tied.

"Yeah," was all that sputtered out. I cleared my throat, wondering if I should press my luck. How could I just take her home when things were going so well? It really was a great night. The stars were out in full force.

"Well, um . . . are you too cold to . . . I mean, I know it's pretty chilly but it's so nice out . . . Would you like to walk as far as the fountains, maybe, before we head back?"

She said she wasn't cold at all.

We walked along toward Town Square, as if we had been going together all year.

I pointed up to the brightest bunch of stars. "That's Orion," I told her. "The Archer."

"Do you know the constellations?"

"Not too many. There're just a few I remember." I went on to tell her about how Andy and Matt and I used to be such astronomy nuts. But I didn't want to bore her with too many details, so I changed the subject.

"Our common hobby nowadays is Conquest."

She looked like she didn't know what I was talking about.

"Oh, I mean . . . see, it's this game," I stammered. "You have a board with a map of this fantasy world, and little tokens for your armies and weapons, and cards to tell you whose side you're on, and . . ." I was starting to sound like a little kid. Maybe I should have stuck to astronomy. So I tried to explain that it wasn't really kid stuff, but I regretted ever mentioning it.

Surprisingly, though, she looked curious. "What kind of fantasy world is it? Past, or future, or—"

I told her a little more about the way it worked but tried to keep it short. I didn't want to spend all my time alone with Julienne talking about a game.

The fountains were shooting up, then falling back toward the pool, all the while lit up by colored lamps hidden in the water. I was breathing in gulps of the cold night air, wondering over the fact that Julienne's hand in mine was making me feel both strong and gentle at the same time.

Just when I was about to actually come out and say something weird like that, she stopped to look at the reflections in the water. And I stopped to look at her.

Quietly watching her as she stared into the water, I wanted to remember for a long time how she looked. Then I saw her lips move, just slightly, into a smile.

"Look at those stars," she murmured, pointing into the pool.

I stepped up beside her to see. Getting too close to her could spoil everything if I wasn't careful. What if I scared her off? What if this wasn't the right place, or time, and what if she didn't feel about me the way I felt about her?

"Do you recognize them?" She was pointing at a bunch of stars mirrored in the water.

Everything caught in my throat. For a minute, "Maybe," was the only sound I made. Because all I could think of was the warm, spicy smell of her hair, and the fact that her right ear was only a few inches away from my lips.

I didn't even consider the consequences. I just started moving. And before I knew it, my lips were right above her ear, near her temple, nestled in her hair.

I pulled away slowly, still only half-aware of what I was doing.

"It's the Winged Horse," I started babbling. "Pegasus."

"It is?" she whispered. With the wind catching her curls and feathering her face with them, she turned toward me and smiled.

Chapter Nine

What I never would have admitted to anyone was that what happened next was, for all practical purposes, my first kiss. The others had all been rushed, goodnight type things, in cars or on doorsteps.

But this one, with just Julienne and me all alone under the stars, really meant something. When I put my hands on her shoulders, she felt so small and fragile that for a second I was worried that she would either run away or break in two. But then, watching her smile, I knew it would be O.K. And kissing her was much more than O.K.—it just about set me on fire.

The main thing was that I had never felt anything like that with anybody else. I thought I could never get enough of just holding Julienne, and feeling her soft lips on mine. But eventually, we sort of gently moved apart and walked on back to the car.

* * *

The next day, I couldn't help wondering just how many times Julienne had kissed before. It had to be a lot. She had fallen into it so naturally that I knew she must have had some practice. Not that the idea bothered me. In fact, it relieved me. Maybe she wasn't as helpless as she sometimes seemed to be. I hoped so. I wasn't used to handle-with-care women. They made me nervous, since it seemed so easy to insult them. I hoped that the sophisticated, wise side of Julienne was the real her. I was doing my thinking as I vacuumed the upstairs hall, one of my regular chores. But I switched off the vacuum when I thought I heard somebody calling me.

"Pete!" my dad yelled. "You can go off duty for a while. You've got some buddies here to see you."

"Yeah. Us." Andy bellowed up.

"You?" I yelled back. "Come on up." I coiled the cord and wheeled the machine to a corner.

Matt and Andy were both shaking their heads as they came up the stairs.

"You're 'on duty' today, huh?" Andy asked in a pitying voice too low for my dad to hear.

"'Man may toil from sun to sun but woman's work is never done,'" Matt said, as if his heart were heavy with great sorrow for me.

I led them into my room, trying to ignore their cracks.

"I'm surprised you guys are even awake. What's up?"

Andy fell onto my bed, making it creak and groan, and propped his hands behind his head. Matt was standing beside the globe by the window, spinning it as fast as it would go, then pointing at random locations to see where he'd land.

I pulled up my desk chair and sighed helplessly. "Look. I'm playing racquetball with my dad in exactly one hour. What do you two goons want?"

"Suspicions, suspicions . . . tsk-tsk-tsk," Matt scolded. "We're your best friends, Pete. Have you no trust?"

I squinted my eyes at him. Now I *knew* they were up to something.

"We just wanted to get a few household tips from you, that's all," Andy claimed innocently, struggling to keep a straight face.

Matt snickered. "How do you keep the vacuum from sucking up the rug?"

"And what's the best stain remover for lipstick? See, I have this terrible—"

"Problem. Girls leave it all over your body." I finished for him. "I've heard this before, Andy. It's not getting any funnier."

"And don't you think you're getting too old for menial jobs like vacuuming, Pete? Shouldn't you be moving up to something like, oh, polishing the silver?"

"No," I said evenly, not even gritting my teeth. "We don't have any silver. And you know, I like vacuuming. It gives me a chance to work out my frustrations. Like, I imagine that each little speck on the carpet is someone I know, and don't happen to like at the moment. Then, *whoof!* They're gone." I smiled pleasantly.

Neither of them said a word. Andy just stared up at the ceiling, and Matt kept spinning the globe. It was like waiting for a bomb to drop.

Finally, it did.

"Happy birthday to you, happy birthday to you . . ." Andy's singing voice was the pits.

Matt looked straight at me. "Did you have fun last night?"

All the blood drained out of me. There it was. I should have guessed.

"Colleen's big birthday party, huh?" Andy wore a sinister grin.

I swallowed hard, trying to think before I spoke. That was not one of my talents. But I had to be careful this time. Getting into this problem any deeper was not something I could afford.

"Well," I began. "See, guys—"

Andy didn't let me go on.

"We saw, all right. You and Miss Mystery Dream Date, out on the town."

Now, all the blood came rushing back, making me uncomfortably hot. "You . . . *saw?*"

"In a manner of speaking," Matt answered calmly. "At least, we know all about it now."

"You do?"

They must have set spies on me. Blair and Stephen! That had to be—

"We know enough," Matt confirmed.

Andy sat up. "We know you weren't at *Colleen's birthday party.*"

"And we know that you went out—" Matt provided.

Andy got in the crucial stab. "—with some girl."

Some girl! I felt like a squirming fish, unhooked and tossed back in the pond. Andy would have said her name if they knew it. They wouldn't pass up a chance to torture me about someone like Julienne Kelsey, for sure.

Matt yawned dramatically. He was trying to act like Sherlock Holmes. "It's out of the bag, Garroway. We called here last night to ask if you remembered how many points away from the six-gun laser Andy was in the last game. He wouldn't take my word for the fact that he still needed fifty. And Colleen told us almost everything we needed to know: (a) you weren't at home, (b) you wouldn't be until late, and (c) that she was surprised you passed up us, your faithful buddies, for a mere date. We were too shocked to ask who with. So who was it, lover boy? Anyone we know?"

I sighed. At least Colleen hadn't blabbed Julienne's name. And now, at least, I wouldn't have to go to all the trouble of confessing on my own. Andy and Matt already knew I had skipped out on them to go out with "a girl." They knew, and didn't seem too shaken up by it. The only trouble was, they weren't going to stop at that. It might take a few days, but sooner or later they'd find out who Miss Mystery Dream Date had been. And then I'd be in for it.

"That's for me to know and you to find out," I said.

Chapter Ten

I couldn't decide if I felt more like a double agent or a person with a split personality. Because over the following week, I had to bounce back and forth between two different lives. One hour I was Garroway, good ol' buddy to a couple of wild and crazy guys, and the next I was Peter, new boyfriend to one beautiful girl. The biggest problem was that there was no mixing the two. I couldn't figure out a way to tell Andy and Matt about Julienne. No time seemed like a good time. They were busy, I was busy—or I was just plain chicken. Things were going so well between Julienne and me that I didn't want anything to flub it up. Andy and Matt were just crazy enough to come out and say something stupid right to her face.

So all the time I spent with her was top secret. And I tried not to mention my friends too much around Julienne either, so that she wouldn't get curious about meeting them.

"See you at lunch," Matt said, when I saw him in the halls Monday morning.

"Hey, no! I won't be there!" I yelled back. "Gotta go home and work."

I didn't *have* to go home and work that week. I had volunteered, telling my parents I needed the extra money. That part was true. There wasn't much Vacation Pet Caretaking to do this time of year. And one thing about my sisters' beliefs I hadn't been able to accept yet was that it was O.K. for a guy to pay only for his own share of dating expenses. With Webber Falls girls, that wouldn't go over too well. I didn't want to try it on Julienne.

Anyway, going home for lunch meant I didn't have to worry about the two parts of my double life coming together in the cafeteria. But I was a nervous wreck whenever Julienne and I were together in public.

On Saturday I played Conquest with the guys as usual. Then, on Sunday night, I asked Julienne to ride the bus with me to Luigi's Pizzeria. The big green county bus crawled along, stopping at just about every intersection to pick up people I knew were going to turn out to be Frazier High spies.

When we came to our stop, I claimed to be catching a cold.

"Let's hurry on and get into the restaurant," I said when we came to our stop. "It's pretty chilly out here."

And just before we went in, I thought I saw Andy's car turn the corner. I made sure we got a booth by the window for lookout purposes.

By the time I got home, I was wiped out. Maybe I really was catching a cold, I thought as I pulled the covers way up over my head. The best thing that could happen would be for me to go into some deep, dreamless sleep for a week and wake up with all these stupid problems solved. Julienne and

Andy and Matt would all come over and meet at my bedside. They would all get to know and appreciate each other, since they would all be so miserably concerned for my welfare.

But none of that happened. When I woke up Monday morning I knew I had to play the whole charade all over again. And it turned my stomach. How much longer was this going to go on? I had to tell my friends about Julienne eventually. Why was I afraid of them, for cripes sake? My oldest buddies? And what was the worst thing they could do about it, anyway?

Razz me. That's all, I realized with a jolt. All they could do was bug me. Endlessly. There were a million other things they never stopped hassling me over—the vacuum, the dishes, even my crazy fit back in fourth grade that had turned us all into buddies to begin with.

So why not add something else to the list?

That night, I called Julienne.

"Hi, there!"

"Hi, Peter." She giggled a little. I imagined her pretty smile, the way her eyes turned up at the corners, her cheeks blushing . . .

"Can you hold on for just a second, Peter?"

Her hand must have gone over the receiver, because all I heard were muffled voices. Maybe she was too busy to talk, I hoped. Maybe I should just forget about this plan for tonight and work on it tomorrow instead. But before I thought up any more reasons to procrastinate, she came back on the line.

"Is this a bad time?" I asked hopefully.

"Absolutely not. I was hoping you'd call. How's your cold?"

"Oh. Much better, thanks." *Do it!* I ordered myself, gulping. "Listen, I have a proposition for you."

"Hmmm. What kind of proposition?" The sound of her voice, so sweet and sexy at the same time, gave me courage.

As carefully as possible, I explained that I thought she might enjoy meeting my friends. Matt and Andy, I told her, were great guys. We could all just go to the movies together. One big, happy family.

"Why?" Julienne was good with those one-word killer questions.

Why?

"I just thought—"

Suddenly I felt rotten about the whole thing. Here I was, forcing her into a situation *I* didn't feel good about. What if Andy and Matt gave her a hard time—or worse, what if they wouldn't talk to her at all? I had seen them clam up around girls before. But she said O.K., so I wrapped up the conversation as fast as possible, before she could ask any more questions.

I called Matt next.

"Um, hi, Matt." My voice had already lost a lot of enthusiasm.

"Hi, Garroway. What's up?"

"Uh . . . we had a pretty good game Saturday, didn't we?"

"It was pretty good. I just wish Andy would quit trying to convince us that he's got enough points to use the six-gun, though."

I chuckled. "You can't blame him for trying to make the game more challenging."

"I guess," he conceded. "Was that all you called about? I've got to get back to this history essay. Extra credit, you know."

"Oh, yeah. Sure. No . . . I just, um . . . had this one other thing I wanted to, sort of, ask you. Andy doesn't have a football game this Friday night, so I wondered how you guys would feel about going to see *Fly by Day* or something."

"Sounds good to me. It's not going to be here past this week. But I'm surprised. I thought you'd have *other* plans for Friday night."

I was steaming, but kept my voice down. "You're a real mind reader, Forster. Know that? I can't put anything past you."

He just snickered.

"Julienne Kelsey's coming with us." There. I'd said it.

There was silence. I was dying to see his face. Then I heard his gasp, which sounded something like a death rattle.

"Julienne . . . Kelsey?"

I'd used the best strategy, I decided. Surprise attack. He was so knocked off his rocker that he could barely talk, which left me free to explain how all he had to do was watch the movie and be his normal, wonderful self. Everything would be fine.

"It's been a long time since I've asked you for a favor," I added. "And don't forget, I went with you to that stupid breakfast thing just for the sake of *your* crush."

"But . . . Julienne Kelsey?"

After we hung up, I was all in gear. Right away, I dialed Andy's number—that familiar seven-digit code I'd had memorized for years. Waiting for him to come to the phone, I tried to think of old favors I could remind him of, like the time I had written out every other line of ten pages of *I will not throw spit balls* for him.

"Hey, Andy. What's going on?"

"Oh, watching T.V. Can't believe my dad won't let us get a video cassette recorder. I missed Bo Derek on a Channel 3 special Saturday while we were playing Conquest. Makes me sick."

"Life is tough," I answered. "And speaking of movies,

how 'bout if we see *Fly by Day* Friday night? To take your mind off not having a game.''

"Hey, great! What time?"

"There's an eight o'clock show. And guess what?"

"What?"

"I'm bringing someone along."

"Yeah?" He sounded suspicious.

"Yeah. Julienne Kelsey."

There was a long pause. I braced myself. He was going to say something, and I knew it was going to be the worst thing he could think of.

"Knock it off, Garroway. You're makin' me sick."

Chapter Eleven

Walking from the parking lot to the movie theater, I was imagining how Andy's and Matt's eyes were going to pop out. Julienne looked terrific. They might give her the cold shoulder, just because they were lunkheads, but she sure wasn't a sight they'd forget.

The problem was that even though she looked so great on the outside, it seemed that what was going on *inside* her head was a different story. She was putting up a great front, smiling and laughing on cue, but she had stared out the window a lot on the drive from her house, and now she was walking as stiff and slow as someone being marched to the gallows.

I couldn't understand what the big deal was. Why were she and Andy and Matt so uptight about just going to a movie? It wasn't as if I had asked them to dance together. Convincing

Andy to go had taken me about half an hour on the phone. But he had gotten over the shock much faster than Matt had.

"Julienne Kelsey?" he had repeated. "This is unreal, Garroway. You've actually been dating *her*?"

I stayed calm. "Listen. I'm not trying to get your seal of approval, Hanes. I'm just asking you to meet the girl and give her a chance."

"But Pete, she's a real space cadet. She walks around like some kinda zombie, and wears those bizarre boots and those hats with feathers."

"Look, Hanes, you're kind of strange yourself, and not half as cute as she is."

That shut him up for a while.

Now, with Julienne trailing just behind me, I walked up to where he and Matt were waiting in line for tickets. I took a deep breath and steeled myself for the moment of truth.

"Hey, guys."

The faces they turned to me were long enough to wrap around the block. Great, I thought. Now I had three depressed people on my hands.

But then, the minute their eyes fell on Julienne, a cold chill went through me. Because suddenly everything changed.

"Um, Julienne, I guess you and Matt here know each other a little from math class." I guided her forward, hoping I sounded cheerful. "And this is Andy Hanes, Mr. Touchdown himself."

Her voice went down to that low, husky, heart-stopping murmur of hers. "Glad to meet you."

I could almost feel the electric crackle in the air.

What bothered me, though, was not the way they were staring at her, but something else I couldn't quite put my finger on. Until Andy made his move, that is.

As smooth as Ricardo Montalban on *Fantasy Island*, he

took her hand in his, bowed slightly, and kissed it. "Such a pleasure."

As if that wasn't enough, Matt got in on the act.

"Delighted," he smiled.

Julienne didn't miss a beat. "The pleasure is mine," she replied with a "Shy Di" smile.

I wasn't jealous. The last thing I'd ever worry about was Julienne falling in love with one of those two goons, or about one of them trying to take her away from me. What I *was* worried about was this completely out of character politeness of theirs, and the way Julienne was lapping it up. What if they were just baiting her? What if they were planning to set her up with all this sweetness and light, then pull the rug out?

I didn't like it.

They rushed to hold open the doors for her and help her into her seat. They stuffed her with popcorn and candy. I couldn't decide if they were treating her more like a little kid or a goddess.

And she loved it. I might as well have not even been there, in fact, until the movie got going. Then, at a sort of scary part, she snuggled closer to me and grabbed onto my hand.

I held it in return, but couldn't bring myself to say anything or even to put my arm around her, the way I usually did. She kept acting like a kid—squealing and giggling all through the movie. She never acted that way when we were alone. Somehow I got the feeling that it was all just part of this stupid game with Andy and Matt.

It made me sick. I didn't see how I could make it through any more time with the three of them together.

On the way to get a pizza after the show, Matt decided to deliver an official review of the movie. Julienne looked fascinated.

"You see, when the Winged Gargantuan swoops down into

the Lomolan's Sacred Hall, it represents the inevitability of time—"

"Yes, I see," she nodded.

Matt never would have gone into such garbage about a goofy movie like *Fly by Day* if Julienne hadn't been there. He wouldn't have bothered just for my benefit, or for Andy's. But he was bending over backwards to impress Julienne. What was even worse was that she agreed with every single stupid thing he said. And she acted as if she never could have thought of any ideas like that on her own.

Even Andy was pretending to be interested. Normally he would have laughed his head off and given Matt a shove or two. But tonight he was a saint. He and Matt both were perfect angels.

What a joke.

Sitting in the restaurant booth with them, I was trying to figure out just why it bugged me so much that they weren't being themselves. Meeting Julienne's eyes a couple of times, I found her looking content. Why couldn't I just let it go at that? After all, weren't things going a lot better than I had expected? No one had clammed up or sulked. Julienne wasn't miserable. Why wasn't I happy that they were getting along?

Somebody broke into my thoughts with the mention of Conquest.

"That advanced player manual could really shape up our game," Andy was saying. "If only Mr. High and Mighty Game Master here would give it a chance."

"Look, Andy," Matt came back. "I've already seen that piece of—" He stopped himself, then gave Andy and me pointed looks. "Oh, well. No need to argue over that now. We can discuss this later."

I was amazed. Matt was actually backing down from a Conquest argument. Impossible. He only did that when he was sick or had to study. Or, as in this case, if there was a "lady" present.

I wanted to clang some sense into his head with the pizza pan. Why couldn't he just act normal around Julienne? Why couldn't he and Andy just treat her like another friend? "You guys are too much—" I started to say.

But Andy interrupted. "Matt's right. Let's talk about it later. We must be boring Julienne."

Then Julienne started gushing about how fascinating Conquest sounded and how interested she was in it.

Suddenly it hit me. That was the answer. If Julienne and Andy and Matt were so into playing this dumb game of acting Lady and Gentlemen, then maybe instead of trying to stop it, I could replace it. With another game.

I smiled wickedly at the thought. Matt and Andy would go bananas if I invited Julienne into our Saturday ritual. But I could just see what would happen. Matt and Andy, astonished. And Julienne, sweeping across the board.

Conquest.

Chapter Twelve

"Well, are you all psyched up for tomorrow night?" I plunked my books down on the lunch table across from Andy.

He squinted at me. "I still can't believe you did that, Garroway."

"Did what?"

"Oh, come off it. You know what I'm talking about." He took a mean bite out of his sandwich.

"The books? Hey, sorry. I didn't know they were in your—"

"You zithead. Conquest is what I'm talking about. Why did you invite Julienne to play?"

I sat down, waiting for Matt, who was just walking up. I might as well face them both.

"Hi, Matt. Have a seat. Help Andy give me the third degree."

"About the game?"

"You bet," Andy confirmed.

I started to unpack my lunch. "Why are you just getting around to this now? You've had all week to gripe, and today, Friday, you decide to launch the attack."

"There hasn't been much we could do about it, has there?" Matt asked, wiping his eyeglasses.

"It was some set-up," Andy grunted.

I had to smile in agreement. It *had* been a great set-up, and I was proud of every minute of it. After Julienne had started asking about Conquest, I had jumped right in with, "There's no reason why you can't come next Saturday and find out for yourself. Isn't that right, Game Master Forster?"

He couldn't refuse right in front of her, and now I had it all arranged. The game would be at my house. And if anything could bring out the real personalities of my three friends, it would be Conquest.

"Well, what do you have to say for yourself?" Matt persisted.

"Does this mean you guys don't want Julienne to play? Just this once, even? I thought you were her self-appointed Sugar 'n' Spice Adoration Society. Last Monday, before she came to sit with us here, you, Andy, said she wasn't as bad as—"

"Shhh!" Matt glared at us. "She's coming!"

Andy lowered his voice. "Listen," he said through his teeth. "She's a nice kid. But you're pushing, Pete. You're really pushing for a—"

"Hello," Julienne said softly, coming up to one end of the table and smiling.

"Hi," Matt answered. He flashed his braces at her.

"Have a seat," Andy offered. "Come on, sit next to Pete here." He clapped me on the back.

"That okay with you, Pete?" she asked, wrinkling her nose and giggling.

The giggling bit was embarrassing, and I wondered how I was going to survive another lunchtime with Princess Julienne and the Princes. Then, when she turned her big brown eyes on me and smiled as if there were no one else in the world, I almost forgave her for everything.

But not quite.

Hanging around at her house Saturday afternoon, I started feeling antsy. It was raining like crazy outside, for one thing. You'd think that after living my whole life in the Pacific Northwest I'd have gotten used to the six billion or so inches of annual rainfall. No go. If anything, I get more and more sick of it every year. I'm just not a rainy-day person.

Then, all of a sudden, Julienne decided to drag me upstairs to her room and shut the door, which made me understandably nervous, considering the fact that her mom was right below us in the living room.

"I've got something for you to *read*, silly," she said. "It's my contest entry in the KWEB radio amateur playwright contest for their Theater Hour."

She was beaming as she handed me a folder. I had never seen her look so excited. For just a second, I was afraid to look at her story. I mean, she wanted an honest opinion. What if I didn't like it? But I remembered what Andy always said about her being Lombardi's favorite student. Anyway, I couldn't imagine Julienne writing anything stupid.

"Twenty-five pages! This must have been a lot of work," I said, looking it over.

"You don't have to read it now, if—"

"No, I'd like to. We have some time to kill before dinner at my house, anyway." The truth was that I was curious to see what it was about.

(Sound: Carriage wheels and horses' hooves)
Reed: Dearest Rebecca, it's been so long . . .
Rebecca: Yes, my darling.

Reed: Let me hold you, my love. I want to blaze a trail of kisses . . .

It went on from there. I wondered if I was getting red. It had been a long time since anything had made me embarrassed enough to do that. But reading over a romantic story written by the girl I felt romantic about was all it took to make my face and neck burn hot.

Still, now I could see why Julienne was always pulling A's in English class. She could really write. But I wondered how she had come up with the love scenes. How did she know all this stuff? Where had she done her research? I couldn't remember leaving a trail of kisses along her milky white throat or sweeping her up into my arms to carry her off. In fact, everything I could remember doing as we said good night on her doorstep or walked along in the park or whatever seemed really dull in comparison. Dull and boring. Was that how she thought of me? How could she possibly think of me any other way when she had guys like Reed to compare me to?

I read on to the end, getting more and more worried about the fact that I was nothing like Reed at all. Maybe that was why Julienne spent so much time staring out the window when she was with me. Quickly, I glanced up at her. And there she was again, staring out the window.

Chapter Thirteen

She perked up a lot during dinner at my house. And so did I.

On the way over, I had asked myself why the heck Julienne would bother to spend so much time with me if she really thought of me as such a dud. I mean, there had to be something that attracted her to me, right? And she hadn't backed away or cringed or anything when I'd gone over and kissed her after reading her play. So I decided to stop feeling inferior to Reed and even to stop worrying about the upcoming game of Conquest. What will be, will be.

After dinner, Julienne and I escaped to the den, where we got a hefty fire going. She crossed her arms and sort of scrunched up her shoulders, as if she had just come in from the cold.

"You have a nice family," she said, staring into the flames.

"They like you, too," I answered. "But I thought maybe

dinner here would be too crazy for you. We're pretty noisy folks."

"No," she murmured. "I like it."

"Well, good. Because Andy and Matt are going to be even noisier."

She wasn't smiling, exactly. She had that quiet, far-off expression, like a purring cat.

Suddenly she turned toward me. "When are they supposed to get here?"

"Andy and Matt? In half an hour. I, um...I thought maybe we could go over some of the Conquest basics, if you want to."

"Oh. O.K."

"Get yourself comfortable while I grab a pencil."

When I turned back around, I found her sunk down right in the middle of my family's oldest, softest sofa, which had swallowed her up. I had to laugh.

"Do you think I'm funny?" she asked, not holding back her grin. Her feet barely reached the floor, and the top of her head came to about the middle of the sofa back.

"Very."

I ducked just in time to miss the pillow she had aimed at my head.

"After all, it is a *throw* pillow," I agreed, lobbing it back at her. Meanwhile, she had launched another one, which hit me square in the gut.

"O.K. You wanna play that way?" I grabbed two big cushions from an armchair, and dove, kamikaze-style, onto the couch, where I trapped her with them.

"No!" she yelped between giggles. "You're smothering me."

"I am?" I let her up for air, which was a big mistake,

because she went straight for my ribs, and tickled with no mercy.

"Uncle!" I surrendered.

"No! You're going to pay, Mr. Garroway!"

She was laughing as crazily as I was when Andy and Matt walked in. There we were, lying in a tangled, hysterical heap on the couch. And there they were, getting ready to march back out.

Julienne scrambled off me and stood up, still giggling.

"Hi, guys," I said, sitting up and running a hand through my hair. "Come on in."

They didn't budge.

"You sure?" Andy asked stiffly. "I mean, we could come back later..."

Matt wasn't even looking at us, but was shifting from foot to foot and staring at the floor.

The evening was not getting off to a great start.

"Come on in," I said. "Let's get going. You bring the board, Matt?" I asked idiotically.

Matt always brings the board. He laid it out on the game table, like a funeral director setting up the flowers.

"This is beautiful," Julienne said, looking over the map of Korlon One, the world we were about to fight over. "These colors—"

Matt jumped right in with an explanation. "Yes. You see, Korlon One is divided into unequal sectors, each represented by a different color. I have two decks of cards here," he went on in a first-grade teacher voice as he started to deal them. "One deck determines your home sectors, and the cards you get from the other deck determines which weapons and power resources you start out with. We're beginning a whole new game tonight, O.K.? So we're all equal."

Julienne nodded. "I'm glad to hear that. Otherwise I'd

never have a chance." She smiled so sweetly that even Andy came out of his grumpy silence.

"Aw, now. It's not that hard. You just watch what we do. We'll help you."

Pretty soon, she started asking questions. I began to relax. Maybe Julienne would enjoy this game, after all. Matt and Andy were already having a great time showing off.

By the time we were all set up, Julienne looked as eager as a kid with new toys. And by her tenth turn, she was on the edge of her chair, with cheeks all flushed and eyes glittering. She examined the board.

"Listen," Matt suggested. "You could get into Pete's Vit sector easily."

"Or I'll even let you tromp into Hannex for a while, so you can get twenty power points," Andy offered gallantly.

She smiled. "Hmmm. Thank you. But I think what I want to do is . . ."

Three pairs of eyes followed her long, gracefully pointed fingers to the middle of the board.

"Quetar Sector attacks Tantin Region."

"Tantin Region!" Andy barked. "You're crazy. That's mine!"

Matt told her, "You can't even attempt to take an entire region unless you've got at least *two* sixth-power-level weapons, and—"

Without a word, she held up not two, but four cards, and showed us her point tally.

I thought Matt was going to have a stroke. His lips turned blue. Andy's whole face turned red, and his eyes started bulging out the way they do when he's about to grab up a lamp and send it air mail express across the room.

I couldn't help it. I cracked up. "Pretty impressive, huh, guys?" I said, trying to break the tension. "Four sixth powers. Not bad for a first time—"

"Not bad!" Andy yelled, jumping up and snatching Julienne's point tally from her hand. "It's impossible!"

"Highly unlikely," Matt echoed.

Julienne was cringing, sinking down low into her chair. "But I've kept track—"

"And so have I!" Matt insisted, checking his chart against hers. "Range Roamer, Laser Zoom—"

"It doesn't matter," Julienne said softly. "I don't have to attack there, if—"

"What do you mean, you don't have to?" Andy demanded. "If you've got the guns, you *have* to, by the rules." He was still bright red. Matt's lips were getting even bluer, and with Julienne sitting there, we had a regular Stars and Stripes. Because she was going white as a sheet.

"Hey, come on, guys," I said, laughing a little, hoping they'd all see how dumb they were acting. "It's not such a big deal. It's just a game."

"Yeah!" Andy shot back. "Just a game. Unless people start cheating."

"Cheating?" Julienne squeaked.

"Cheating?" I croaked.

"Yeah, cheating," Andy answered, watching Matt, who was still hunched over his charts.

"Highly unlikely, highly unlikely," he kept muttering.

I couldn't believe they were putting on such a big production. I didn't feel like laughing anymore. I felt like punching their faces in. But I didn't have a chance to do it.

"I don't cheat!" Julienne cried suddenly, jumping out of her chair so fast it almost fell over.

Matt looked surprised for a second, then made his face a blank. "Then how could you possibly do so well so soon?"

She was trembling and chalk white. "I just played. By your rules."

I touched her arm. "Why don't we just calm down. This isn't such a big—"

She yanked away from me. "Calm down?" Her lower lip was trembling.

I knew it. She was going to cry.

"Good night!" she sputtered, and ran out of the room.

"Julienne!" For a minute, yelling that out was all I could do. I felt paralyzed. I'd asked for it, hadn't I? I'd wanted to bring out the real personalities of my friends, and I'd succeeded.

"Great game, huh, Garroway?" I heard Andy say. "It's always fun to play with girls."

"Well, aren't you going to run out after your little love-dove?" Matt wanted to know.

To keep from knocking all their teeth in, I did run out.

She was halfway to her house by the time I caught up with her.

"Julienne, wait!"

She whirled around so fast that I nearly barreled right over her. I caught her in my arms just in time. And that was when I saw it written all over her face. In the dim streetlight I saw the angry twist of her mouth and the way her eyebrows were pulled together so hard that they almost met in a straight line over her nose.

"Julienne," I began, "those two were just acting up. You shouldn't let them get to you."

"Get to me! Peter, they—they—" She was shaking all over. "I don't cheat!"

"Heck, I know that, Julienne. Of course you don't. But that's not the point. They just—"

"They raked me over the coals!"

I couldn't stand to see her that way. Just wait till I get my hands on those clods, I thought. I was ready to take Matt and Andy apart for doing this to her. In the meantime, I tried to comfort her with a hug, but she wouldn't let me. She was really wound up.

"Andy and Matt are like that, Julienne." I tried to sound reassuring, so she'd quiet down. "They're not worth crying over."

Suddenly I got the idea that she should be hearing this from them, not me. They should tell her they were sorry.

"Listen. Let's go back and get them to apologize, and just forget the whole thing."

It backfired.

"Go back?"

"Well," I said. "Sure. They'll come to their senses."

I held my breath, wondering whether the look on her face meant she was about to let loose another stream of tears or sock me in the jaw.

Her voice was almost a whisper. "I won't go back there tonight, Peter."

I let my breath go. "Yeah, O.K. I can understand that. But you've got to know, Julienne, that the way they acted tonight was nothing personal."

"Then you don't understand yet, do you?" She shook her head. "Andy and Matt have never liked me. They were just acting nice for—for your sake. Can't you see that they wanted to drive me out tonight? They want someone better for you."

"Someone better?" I looked hard at her, trying to see if she was serious. She was. And when she brought up the rotten way I'd acted every time Matt and Andy were around, I cringed, feeling guilty—a vampire getting a stake through the heart. She was right. I had been pretty stupid.

Then she drove the stake even deeper. "You wanted to get their approval," she accused me. "That's why you've been forcing us all together."

I drew the line there. "No! Hold on a minute. I don't need their approval for anything."

"Then why did you insist on getting us all together, when it was clear that they couldn't stand me?"

I tried to convince her she was wrong about them hating her, but she wouldn't believe it.

"What happened tonight, then?" she asked. "Why did they gang up on me?"

I took a deep breath and tried to explain everything as honestly as I could. How I had wanted my friends to like her and accept her. And how they really had changed their minds about her once they got to know her. Then I got to the hard part.

"The reason they blew up tonight is because—" I knew I was going to have to bring it all out, but how would she take it? Would it make her fall apart again?

"It has to do with the way you played Conquest."

"The way I . . ." She looked stunned. "But I was trying so hard to do well, to please them!"

"You did do well. It was pretty darned impressive. And that was the problem."

Thinking back to how crude Andy and Matt had been to her, I felt my face and neck heating up with anger.

"I hate to say it, Julienne, but my friends, those lunkheads I grew up with, are real male chauvinist pigs. When it comes down to it, they . . . See, they didn't like it when you did so well. They've still got this idea that girls really shouldn't be as competitive and everything as guys, and when you started beating them at their own game, they went nuts."

The thought of how shocked they had been was making me feel good. For once, Andy and Matt had really been thrown off their high horses. That feeling must have come out in a smile on my face, because Julienne suddenly looked pretty mad.

"Do you think that's funny?" she asked.

71

"No—oh, listen, I'm sorry." I realized she thought I was laughing at her. "What I'm happy about is how good you got them. You really stuck it to them tonight with that maneuver. They need to be shaken up like that more often."

Apparently, that was not what she wanted to hear.

"Peter, I was not trying to shake anyone up. I just . . . I thought"—she was shivering again—"I thought I was doing what they wanted, and what you wanted. But you always seemed so upset around them, and then tonight—"

"O.K.," I interrupted. I was going to have to give her all the answers. So I confessed to setting up the Conquest game to teach Matt and Andy a lesson—and to show Julienne what they were really like.

"Do you mean," she said softly, "that you actually *planned* for Andy and Matt to turn on me?"

I could see that my explanation hadn't done much good, and I probably should have stopped then before things got even worse. But I went right on explaining. I told her how I had known that a good game of Conquest would make Andy and Matt stop holding her up on a pedestal, and that it would let her come down off it.

I may have been imagining it, but I thought I felt her shoulders tense up under my hands.

"What . . . pedestal?"

"Well . . . take your story, for instance." I stalled for a second, then forged ahead, all systems go. "What bothered me about it is that you've got the heroine, Rebecca, who is perfectly intelligent and capable. But the hero, Reed, is always having to come along and rescue her from all kinds of things. It's a great story, but life doesn't happen that way, Julienne."

I tried to be careful, so that she wouldn't think I was making fun of her. I could tell that talking about her story had been the wrong thing to do. But my mouth kept moving. I told her that she acted as if life was a fairy-tale world and that she shouldn't have fallen for the way Matt and Andy had treated her at first.

"At least they were nice to me then!" she protested.

"Maybe it seemed that way," I said as gently as I could. "But remember, they were only nice while you acted like a little fairy-tale princess."

Her eyes were still puffy, but she wasn't crying anymore. She was just staring at me, focusing those big brown eyes right on mine like a bomber zeroing in on the target.

"So you set this all up? You deliberately set up that game just to teach me a lesson about life?"

She was definitely getting the wrong idea.

"Julienne, I didn't mean for you to get hurt." I was still hoping she'd see it all my way.

"Why didn't you just come out and *tell* me how you felt?"

Well, why hadn't I? *There must be a reason,* I told myself.

"Would you have listened?" I finally asked. "You seemed so taken in by Andy and Matt that I didn't think warning you would do any good."

"I see." Her voice had gone so flat that it gave me goose bumps. "You just decided to conduct a harmless little experiment, with me as the guinea pig. A shy, mixed-up girl—the perfect subject—used to teach your friends a thing or two, as well!"

The goose bumps spread all the way up to my scalp. "It wasn't like that, Julienne. You don't understand. I just wanted to help you."

It was probably the worst thing I could have said.

"I don't need that kind of help," she hissed. "What I need is—is—"

"Julienne, please. Listen."

"Listen to what? More of your preaching?"

There were no goose bumps now. I was in a cold sweat.

"You have no right to try to change me, Peter!" She was crying full force now.

"But that's not what I was trying to do, Julienne! I was—I was—"

Suddenly, I didn't know anymore what I was trying to do. My mind went blank on that great plan I'd had for everybody. All I could see was Julienne standing on the sidewalk, glaring at me.

"Oh!" she cried suddenly, burying her face in her hands. "Just leave me alone!"

She turned around, ran into her house and slammed the door before I could say it.

I'm sorry.

Chapter Fourteen

I hit the ball so hard that it ricocheted from the front wall to the left wall, then bounced off a lamp on the ceiling. My dad crouched there in his faded gym shorts and worn-out racquetball shoes, staring at the front wall.

I took off my safety glasses. "You won the set."

"True, but you played pretty well, considering how tense you seem to be. Something sure is distracting you, isn't it?"

"You could say that." He didn't ask me what. I just followed him out of the concrete-block racquetball court to the locker room. Something was more than distracting me. The thought of how hard Julienne had cried, of how I had stormed back to my house and yelled at Andy and Matt to leave, was killing me. Worst of all was that I knew I had brought it all down on myself. I'd pushed everyone too far.

"Hmmm. We've got the whole place to ourselves this

morning," Dad said, jumping into the shower. "I can sing anything I want. Aïda, Rigoletto—"

"Not today, Dad."

"Hey, something's really eating at you, isn't it?" He had his eyes squeezed tight on account of the shampoo trickling down his forehead. "Wanna talk?" he asked.

I shrugged and started to towel off. "I dunno. Seems like a hopeless case."

"Huh?" he grunted, shaking the water out of his hair like a sheepdog. "You, the ultimate optimist, call anything hopeless? Ridiculous!"

"It's not ridiculous. It's a mess. And I don't know where to start straightening it out."

"Too personal to tell me what it is?" he asked.

"Not in general." I fished around in my athletic bag for my socks. "I mean, what can be personal about your ex-best friends and your ex-girlfriend?"

"Uh-oh. I hear trouble."

"Big trouble," I agreed. "Everyone's mad at me. First, Julienne walked out on us. Then I chased Andy and Matt out."

"You did? Why?"

"They're idiots. That's why. They really hurt Julienne. And then I ended up hurting her, too. It's so mixed up . . ."

"Take it from the top," Dad prompted.

I sighed and plunked myself down on the bench. "O.K. I'll start with Andy and Matt. The way they treat girls is just unreal. I mean, they can't just talk to girls—especially girls our own age. They've got to set up all these little games and act super-polite. Stuff they'd never do for another guy. For days they treated Julienne like some kind of princess. As long as she was sweet and prissy, everything was fine. But as soon as she showed a little spunk and started winning last night during the Conquest game, *poof!* They turned on her like wolves.''

"Sounds bad," Dad agreed. "But can't you see how Andy and Matt have been handicapped by their environment? By advertisements, by jokes, by the movies . . . They weren't *born* afraid of women, you know.''

"Afraid?" I was totally confused.

"Listen, Pete. You grew up in a house full of women and girls with strong personalities. Maybe your friends didn't have that advantage. All their lives they've probably heard that girls should be sweet and prissy, and girls shouldn't be too assertive or too intelligent. When females don't fall into the right categories, I'll bet Andy and Matt get worried. They don't know what to think or how to act. It's scary for them to cope with real live girls.''

"You think so?"

Dad shrugged. "Could be. You know your friends better than I do. Think about it.''

I did. Constantly. On Monday I walked home for lunch. The cold November winds helped clear my head. My parents didn't need me on the phones, but I just didn't want to be at school any more than was absolutely necessary.

On one hand, I was mad at all of them—Andy, Matt, and Julienne. On the other, I had never felt so lonely. There were plenty of other guys who'd make good buddies and plenty of other girls who'd been on my mind way before I'd ever seen Julienne Kelsey. But it wouldn't be the same. Especially not since I had this nagging guilt hanging around.

Trying to finish my homework Monday night, I asked myself some questions. Who was the big shot who had decided to "get everybody together?" Who was the one who *knew* that Matt and Andy could get crazy around girls, but went ahead and made Julienne go out with them, anyway?

Was it really my friends' fault that they were such pigheads? Just like my dad said, weren't they just programmed by the world around them? I couldn't expect them to get deprogrammed overnight. It seemed that I had managed to hurt them just as much as they had hurt me. And Julienne. Just saying her name out loud made my eyes sting a little. The memory of how she had looked out there on the sidewalk Saturday night, so miserable and mad . . . It made me want to call her up right away. It made me want to tell her how stupid and sorry I was. But just as clearly, I remembered what she had said. *Leave me alone.*

Right then, the phone rang, jolting me back to the fact that I had one more math problem to do.

My mom's voice calling up the stairs took care of that. "Peter, it's Andy."

I just about ran to the phone.

Chapter Fifteen

Within fifteen minutes of that call, I was in Andy's car on the way across town to Matt's house.

"What the heck is going on, Hanes? I sure wish you had said more than 'Matt's in bad shape' over the phone."

"Hey, calm down." I couldn't. "My little sister was right there, and my parents were in the next room. I couldn't blab out Matt's love life with all of them listening."

"Matt's love—" I felt all my adrenalin settling down.

"Hey, it's nothing to laugh about, Pete, ol' buddy. Matt's in ba-ad shape."

"What do you mean, he's in bad shape? He's in traction, or what?" I was beginning to feel almost O.K. again. This was like old times. All forgotten; no questions asked. I didn't want to bring up the way he'd accused Julienne of cheating and made her cry or any of the other stuff. I wanted to start over.

"You'll see," Andy said. "Poor guy's really worked himself up. Barely talks, barely eats. Looks like he hasn't slept in years. It's over Delacorte."

"Delacorte?" Suddenly it started making sense to me. "Heck. No wonder."

"No wonder what?"

"The way he's been acting in chem lab. Like a zombie. I thought he was just . . . well, you know. Julienne, and all."

"Nah. It's not that." Andy looked me right in the eye.

Before I could think of a comeback, he said, "Anyway, we've gotta do something to bring him out of this. Could be fatal. He's such a skinny little bag o' bones already, he can't afford to starve himself. And you know what he did?"

I imagined the Northside Bridge at midnight.

"Flunked a history test."

My jaw dropped. "He what? Matt's never flunked *anything*!"

Andy shook his head. "Times are a-changin'."

When we got to the Forsters', Matt was in his room hunched over his history book, staring at it the way a condemned man stares at pictures of his family.

"Hey, Matt ol' buddy." Andy clapped him on the back.

Matt didn't even look at him.

"You two think you're funny, don't you?"

I could hardly believe he had said anything, and just froze.

"Whaddya mean, we think we're funny?" Andy asked, frowning. "Sure we are. Hey, Pete? Hear the one about the frog that—"

"I don't want to hear any more of your jokes, Hanes. I've had plenty."

Now Andy was a statue. I just kept my mouth shut and

stared from one face to the other. Matt's was red and furious.

"Real funny. Hah, hah, hah," he sneered. "Let's have a good laugh on little ol' Matt, shall we? Let's make him do his tricks."

"Aw, Matt," Andy offered. "Look, it wasn't anything like that. You know I—"

"I know you'll do anything to entertain yourself, Hanes. And you . . ." He shot a glare at me.

"Me?" I was shocked.

"Why don't you guys just go pick on someone else."

"Hey, man," I said. "We're trying to help you out. What makes you think we're picking on you?"

But Matt was too far gone to answer my question. He just kept on talking like he was in a trance. "Do you know what she said, Hanes? Do you know what she said? She said, 'Matthew. Dear Matthew. This is touching. Really quite touching. But we're such good friends. Let's keep it that way.' And she handed the note back to me, resealed, as if she hadn't even read it."

My mouth jumped into action. "You gave her a *note*?"

"Yes," he confessed, still glaring at me. "In that note I wrote all I'd ever wanted to say to her, exactly the way you suggested."

"I . . . me?" I had to sit down. Somehow I felt I had just crossed into the Twilight Zone.

"I wasn't going to do it, Garroway. But when *he* told me that you had said I should . . ." He turned his glare on Andy.

"Hey now, Matt. That wasn't exactly what—"

I had a strong desire to stuff them both into the nearest carrot-juicer.

"Will you guys tell me what the heck you're talking about?" So they did. And we had a long talk.

By the time I got home, I was worn out, but too keyed up

to sleep. Now I had one problem solved. All that explaining had cleared the air with my friends.

"I never meant to laugh at you, Matt," Andy had insisted. "It was just that I was sick of seeing you chase around after Delacorte, and never get anything out of it. That happens to guys all the time, and girls never bother to straighten them out. I knew the only cure was the hard one—getting her to tell you herself."

"Appreciate your kindness," Matt had muttered.

"See what I mean?" I said. "The same thing happened with Julienne. You guys were putting her on this pedestal, and when she decided to come down off it for a while, you couldn't handle it."

I guess they were too beat to argue. Because to my total surprise, they mumbled that they were sorry.

We were buddies again. Maybe they weren't going to be just the way I wanted them. But the important thing was that they weren't going to hassle me anymore about Julienne. They were going to accept her as part of my life.

And that was my next problem. Was Julienne still willing to play that part?

I piled into bed and turned on the radio.

"And now for KWEB Accu-Weather . . . we'll have a low of thirty-six degrees tonight under cloudy . . ."

The announcer had a low, dreamy voice, a lot like Julienne's. I wondered if she also had a pair of eyes like Julienne's. Impossible.

"Tomorrow is expected to be fair, but windy, with a high of fifty-eight and a low of—"

I wondered if she had anything like Julienne's long, fire-colored hair. No way.

"It's one o'clock now. And just for you listeners who might have missed the announcement earlier, I have the Theater Hour winners list to—"

Did this announcer smell like apples and trees and—
Suddenly, I bolted up. *Theater Hour!*

"And, finally, for our third-place winner . . . Webber Falls'
own . . . Julienne Kelsey."

Chapter Sixteen

I didn't sleep all night. Too many things were buzzing through my head. There was the number one problem—how to get back to Julienne. I had to somehow get her to let me within sight of her again. Number two problem was how to go about congratulating her. She deserved a big celebration for winning that writing contest. And then there was number three—how to convince her that I had changed. I would never again try to force her and Matt and Andy on each other. In fact, I hoped I would never again try to force anything on anyone.

I couldn't believe I had been such a lunkhead. When I told Julienne she should look at life more realistically, I should have taken my own advice. It wasn't fair to demand that Andy and Matt change overnight or that Julienne see things exactly the way I wanted her to. Life just didn't work out that way.

What *was* going to work out was Julienne and me. I was determined.

The result of that night of brainstorming was that at four o'clock the next afternoon, I was at Briar Grove Stables trying to rent the slowest, oldest, most laid-back horse they had.

"You haven't ridden before?" the pretty blond woman asked.

I glanced nervously out the window of the shed to make sure Julienne was still in the training ring, taking her lesson.

"Uh, no, I haven't, and I don't plan to today, either. See, this is, uh, sort of a special occasion."

"Oh? What kind?"

"Well . . ."

After hearing the rest of my plan, the woman agreed to let me hide behind the shed with a big old horse named Ranger until Julienne was through.

Everything would have been just fine, with me standing there holding Ranger's reins in one hand and a bouquet of daisies in the other, if it hadn't been for the fact that he was not exactly the kind of horse I'd had in mind. He was old, all right. He had a spotted gray coat and wise-looking face. Since Vacation Pet Caretaking hadn't included experience with horses, I didn't want to take on more than I could handle. I wanted a nice, gentle nag. But this old geezer was anything but gentle. He kept throwing his head around and stomping and whinnying at the top of his lungs. It was a temper tantrum, if ever I'd seen one. He wanted the daisies.

So I had to hold on to his reins while trying to keep the daisies away from his big, yellow chompers. By the time the woman in the shed finally gave me my cue, I was a wreck.

"Julienne," I heard her ask, "are you going out the main gate?"

That was it. I couldn't see Julienne yet, but I heard her say yes, and knew that at any minute she was going to be visible on the gravel path that led out to the street. It was time for me to start sneaking out there.

Very soon, I learned that sneaking is not easy with a giant, four-legged brat in tow. At first Ranger refused to budge. Then he wanted to go back to his stall. Finally I stuck a daisy out in front of his nose and started pulling. He followed.

One by one, the daisies were snarfed. And step by step, we got closer to Julienne. Her hair, in one long braid, swung back and forth between her shoulders like a pendulum. The sight of it was enough to make my throat tighten up with wanting her back again.

Things were going just fine, with me leading the old horse and Julienne just a few yards ahead of us. But I guess I must have gotten carried away with thinking about her and forgotten to give Ranger his daisies, because all of a sudden he stopped dead in his tracks and belted out one of those earthshaking whinnies.

That, of course, made Julienne turn around.

It wasn't supposed to happen that way. I was supposed to call out to her myself in an impressive baritone, and win her back with my own personal charm. Ranger was stealing the show.

For a long time Julienne stared at him, barely giving me a passing glance. There was no hint of a smile or frown or anything to show that she even recognized me. It was like she had spent a month dating the stupid horse, not me. Either that, or she still wanted me to leave her alone. I didn't wait to find out.

"My dearest Lady Julienne," I began, "whose lovely name I have heardeth on the radio. My dearest, most brilliant contest winner." It sounded a lot more dumb now than it had when I practiced it last night. But it was too late for changes.

Kneeling at her feet, I tried to look as much like a valiant knight as I could, considering I felt like a total idiot.

"In humble apology for the unpardonable antics of my boorish, oafish associates, as well as for my own demented ravings, I am most humbly devoted to your——"

Ranger picked that particular second to swoop his ugly mouth down right into the few daisies I had left. He munched all the heads off before I could even untangle myself from his reins.

"Why, you——"

I stopped without saying what I had in mind, only because I was supposed to be a courtly knight. Feeding Ranger the stems to keep him quiet, I cleared my throat.

"I am most humbly devoted to your service, fair lady. At your command, at your whim, and at your beck and call, I am yours."

What I did next was not in the script. It was just a kind of sudden inspiration. I took her silky-soft hand and pressed it, palm upward, to my lips the way Reed did with Rebecca's in Julienne's story.

It was the crucial moment. If I hadn't gone too far already with the horse and the kneeling and the speech, I knew that kissing her hand would either make or break my whole plan.

Even when she started giggling, I wasn't sure. Not until I looked up and saw her wrinkling her nose and blushing did I know that everything was going to be O.K.

But before I even had a chance to feel relieved, she seemed to collapse. It scared the daylights out of me. I didn't realize at first that she wasn't fainting, but was kneeling, right in front of me, still holding my hand.

"Sir Peter, oh noble lord."

I couldn't believe it.

"Both honored and dismayed am I by your plea," she went on, " 'twas I—oh! 'twas I, m'lord, who taxed you, who tormented and provoked you. Nay, you must never again speak of suffering guilt!''

The way she was looking down and shaking her head had me convinced. I was falling into the fantasy with her.

"Nay!" I said. "I shall, fair Julienne. For I—'' Then it hit me that this had gone on long enough. I'd gotten her attention, I'd gotten her to laugh, but now I wanted to be Peter talking to Julienne. "For cripes sake, Julienne, I've got to talk normal for a minute,'' I said. "You're too important to me to let you go so easily,'' I told her, keeping my eyes on hers. "You told me to leave you alone, so, like a fool, I did. But last night when I heard you had won the contest, I couldn't stay away anymore. I acted like a jerk, Julienne. Andy and Matt acted like jerks. And you were right. I had no right to try to change you three, in the first place.''

For a while, we didn't move a muscle, but just held hands and took each other in.

"But I could use some changing,'' she murmured. Her eyes were glimmering.

"I want you the way you are, Julienne. I always have. Ever since you first came to Frazier last year, I've been thinking about you.''

She looked amazed—and happy. "You have?''

"Yes, ma'am.'' I had to let her know how I felt. "I'm really sorry about putting you through the ringer with Andy and Matt. Honest. I never thought they'd get that rowdy.'' I tried explaining again, and I don't think I did a very good job. But Julienne must have been ready to forgive me, because she was smiling, and once, when I told her what chickens Matt and Andy really were, she even laughed.

She seemed to be feeling a lot better, but her next question came in a quiet, hesitant voice.

"Peter, you're not just interested in me as, well, someone to—''